A Kind of Fiction

A Kind of Fiction

P.K. Page

The Porcupine's Quill

CANADIAN CATALOGUING IN PUBLICATION DATA

Page, P.K. (Patricia Kathleen), 1916–
A kind of fiction

ISBN 0-88984-220-5

1. Title.

PS8531.A34.K56 2001   C813'.54   C2001-930367-X
PR9199.3.P33K56 2001

Published by The Porcupine's Quill,
68 Main Street, Erin, Ontario N0B 1T0.
Readied for press by John Metcalf; copy-edited by Doris Cowan.
Typeset in Bauer Bodoni, printed on Zephyr Antique laid,
and bound at The Porcupine's Quill Inc.

Represented in Canada by the Literary Press Group.
Trade orders are available from General Distribution Services.

We acknowledge the support of the Ontario Arts Council,
and the Canada Council for the Arts for our publishing program.
The financial support of the Government of Canada
through the Book Publishing Industry Development Program
is also gratefully acknowledged.

1   2   3   4   •   03   02   01

Canada

To the memory of the members of *Preview*,
the little magazine where my earliest stories appeared.

————

Grateful thanks
to Théa Gray and Arlene Lampert who read and read

and to Farouk Mitha
whose computer skills spared me a great deal of work.

Table of Contents

A Kind of Fiction

Veronika saw the old woman fall. She couldn't prevent it. She was as helpless as if she were falling herself. She felt with excruciating clarity the old woman's foot slip inside her shoe, saw her pitch forward, extend her arms, and crash down the steps. Slow motion. The sight was horrifying.

Veronika was there when the old woman lay extended on the driveway. 'If I can get her up,' Veronika thought, 'we'll know how badly she is hurt – whether or not she needs to go to emergency.' Veronika didn't like the responsibility. Wasn't sure she would know what to do if the old woman's leg were broken, or her collar bone or hip. Wasn't this the sort of thing that happened to old bones? They grew brittle and cracked.

And these must be old bones. Veronika guessed her to be in her late sixties. She watched as the old woman slowly pushed herself into a sitting position; noticed the quite beautifully set moonstone ring on her engagement finger. Veronika thought the old woman behaved as if she were entirely alone in the world – unobserved. As if the driveway on which she had fallen led only to an empty street in an empty city. In fact, except for Veronika, there *was* no one about. The old woman looked dazed. Veronika wondered if she had suffered a slight concussion or a small stroke for she didn't seem to be aware of Veronika.

She was talking to herself. 'Hurt,' she said, and then, 'Badly?' she asked herself as she stretched each leg – her stockings in ribbons. Her expensive shoes were Italian, Veronika thought. She felt she had seen her before somewhere. At the symphony or on the bus. Veronika couldn't be sure which, and as she continued observing she felt the old woman had a slightly familial look. Would her mother have looked like that if she had lived so long?

The old woman rubbed her shins and then, slowly again, got to her feet, shrugged her shoulders, turned her head from side to side, testing. Veronika noted the excellent cut of her coat.

She noted again that the old woman seemed unable to see her. Didn't want to see her perhaps. Who enjoys such moments of humiliation? Veronika watched her take a step, then another, and set off down the street, slow, but very erect.

* * *

It was some months before Veronika saw her again. Actually saw her. She had dreamed of her often enough and thought of her daily. Had become quite disproportionately preoccupied with her. She was leaving an afternoon concert. Alone. Using a cane. And moving carefully. Veronika wanted to speak to her, but as before the old woman didn't seem to see her, seemed in fact to give her powers of invisibility. Powers she didn't necessarily want.

Veronika followed, on the verge of speech, but somehow silenced. What could she say? 'I've seen you before?' 'I hope you're OK?'

Preferably, perhaps,'Did you enjoy the concert?' Less personal. But Veronika knew the old woman had enjoyed the concert, had a feeling for this music as she herself did. Perhaps the old woman had played the violin in her youth, even performed the difficult Beethoven B flat quartet they had both just heard. Veronika felt she knew what the old woman had thought of the performance. Could she, by some form of thought transference, get into the old woman's mind? If she were to say, 'What did you think of the *presto?*' would the old woman reply that it should have been played faster? Veronika thought she would.

Even so, she felt it would be an impertinence to speak to her. There was a kind of inviolability about the old girl – an impenetrability, perhaps. Veronika felt she actually knew the old woman from the inside – knew her self-containment, knew it was not an aloofness, as many might think, but a mask for a too-warm nature which, in her own best interests, she had to control and direct.

Who were her friends? Veronika wondered. Elderly women, for the most part, as women usually outlive men. Gardeners, probably. Or were they faceless companions found on the Internet? It would not surprise her if the old woman had a computer. Even though most of her generation hadn't. She looked, in a kind of a way, contemporary.

Veronika, lost in her ruminations, suddenly realized that the old woman had disappeared, or that she had misplaced her, the way she misplaced papers on her desk. She must have caught a bus, or picked up a cruising cab, for she was nowhere on the street, though she had been in full sight only minutes before.

So easily and completely had she disappeared that Veronika began to wonder if she had imagined her. But why, under heaven, would she imagine such a person? Surely if she were capable of inventing, she would have invented the perfect companion – male, antic, musical; someone who would make her laugh, pour her a drink when she was tired, draw her a bath. No, she could not, would not, have invented her.

She had read somewhere that characters in fiction very often took on lives of their own, got out of hand and surprised their creators. She had never quite believed that. But she was in no position to argue now. For that was exactly what was happening. The old woman was a kind of fiction, one she could not erase from her mind, one who was absorbing more and more of her time and thought. One who had a provenance. A history. And Veronika knew it, was privy to it in some way she could not understand but which interested her deeply.

Perhaps she should see a shrink, Veronika thought, in parenthesis. For surely this was not a normal preoccupation – but then, what was? – get right down to it. Just *exactly* what was?

Veronika knew the old woman was comfortably off – or had been once, at any rate, before inflation. And married – most certainly. But what did he do – the husband? Veronika questioned briefly. Was he not away most of the time? That perhaps accounted for the children – a girl and a boy. Outrageous children. The girl had been stage-struck since her first school play and, to everyone's surprise had, in her teens, been cast in a production of *Hair*, mainly because – it was commonly thought 'that girl would do anything!' – she had been perfectly willing to stand on stage bare naked, something her mother had not been overly enthusiastic about, but neither had she been exactly shocked or critical, having known her daughter 'from the egg', as it were. Unlike Trik, who had been affronted – darkly affronted. Their son, on the other hand, was a right-wing journalist and that she had found far harder to contend with. It hadn't occurred to her that rebellion would take such a form. Rebellion was surely a swing to the left, or so it had been in her day. So when he had supported the extreme right – publicly, in his column – she had had difficulty discussing it with him. And when his columns became bigoted, prudish, fundamentalist even, it was painful for her – exceedingly painful, as if she herself had made a humiliating *gaffe*.

Jimmy had been quieter than Sylvie – taken to books as other boys take to baseball, despite Trik's valiant efforts to play catch with him, take him camping. That male-bonding that had become so popular and, in some way, so phony. Not that Trik had been phony. He had genuinely wanted to play with his son, but Jimmy had other interests. He wanted Superman comics, but more than those, he wanted children's histories about the furtrade or the wreck of the Titanic. They thought he might take a history major but he took political science and got a night job on a newspaper while still at college. They hadn't worried about Jim the way they had about Sylvie. He was unlikely to take drugs or stay out all night or do any of the things that Sylvie was almost certain to do – once, at any rate.

But neither child had turned out quite as expected – not for *her*, Veronika, for what could *she* expect? – but for the old woman and her dead husband who had dreamed it differently. And now that Trik was dead – yes, Veronika said, that was the husband's name without any doubt – it was not the first time she had said it – now that Trik was dead and she couldn't discuss it with him, or look at it with his objectivity, for he was discerningly objective in the realm of ideas – it was difficult indeed. Although, Veronika thought, the old woman had lived long enough to have seen much diversity in her life and was sufficiently knowledgeable to know how huge the gene pool was, she felt sure that – what? Her mind was wandering.

Veronika, on her way home, and walking along dreamily in her fiction-writing mode – (a mode she had never explored before, and why now? she asked herself) – knew all this about the old woman, and more, even more, when she could keep her mind on it. That was the key – keeping her mind on it – as members of the family created themselves for her, seemingly as fast as they could. She was in no way their puppeteer, their activator, could not have changed a hair on their heads – although Sylvie had done so over and over, dying her blond hair black or red or green – and now she was never to do so again. Dead – flying too close to the sun, drag racing, of all things. Suddenly Veronika shook with sobs. As if Sylvie were her child – bright, gilded, now ash-blackened and gone. Unbearable. She thought of her at kindergarten, like quicksilver on the green grass, so far ahead of all the others. Had she been programmed for attention? Needing it so badly and getting it wherever she went. Shining. Buttercups, she thought. And couldn't bear it.

Veronika wept unashamedly as she walked, burdened by grief – the loss of Trik, of dazzling Sylvie – who had stamped her feet as a child when they called her Syllie – Jimmy's attempt at her name. Veronika felt suddenly weak, barely able to walk, and her head was flooded with them all, such a crowd walked with her – Trik, beloved Trik, and silver Sylvie and Jimmy, poor, poor Jimmy whom she loved – indeed, loved dearly, but loved from the stone heart he had created for her – and why? Oh why? Oh why?

She was dizzy and almost falling, her face wet from weeping. They jostled her – Trik and the two children – Sylver Diamond (stage name); James Ormond (by-line). She had not invented them – Trik, Jimmy and Sylvie – or their real names – Patrick, James and Sylvia. Those were their legal names, their baptismal names. She knew them all as if they were members of her family. But the old woman – the old woman had been nameless. Veronika felt so weak she had to lean against a railing for support. She wondered if she were ill, gravely ill. Then suddenly as if struck by lightning, she knew the old woman's name. It was Veronika. Veronika Sylvia Ormond. Her own.

(2000)

Fever

Baroque furniture, the colour of cinnamon bark. Black-and-white drawings – di Cavalcanti's line as wide as if done with his little finger. Portinari's small purl-purl-purl on thin needles. It is all of a piece with his house but disconcerting to find it here in his office where we must talk, once again, of my uterus. I had thought that finished. The di Cavalcanti seated nude is drawn in an almost continuous line.

Why are we sitting here hand in hand? How did it happen? Did he see my hand across a mile of air or was it close, almost already in his? If it was taken, without my knowledge, why is it now so difficult to withdraw? The two hands play together as we talk – much as children play, separate from their mothers having tea. Playing so prettily that withdrawal becomes a kind of surgery. Not painful – not painful at all. Just violent.

It is done. Without looking. Disengaged.

I know that hand of his as well as one of my own. It is firm, unfleshy – oval nails large in proportion to the fingers. I've seen it so many times changing my dressings, pressing liquid out of the small drain – that practically colourless tube so like the veins one finds in liver.

His hands were surer than the nurse's and so, hurt less. 'Gentler than a woman's.' Such phrases do not belong to this world, this modern world where women are wanting to be men.

The examining room has a bed in it. A bed, not a table. Baroque. Single. It has a scarlet leather mattress and a small green pillow. (And beautiful 'purple shoes with crimson soles and crimson linings,' if I correctly remember my *Little Black*

Sambo.) Two sheets folded and very white.

'Will you help yourself. I have no nurse today.'

'What do you want me to take off?'

'Everything.'

'Everything?' This is absurd.

I took trouble getting dressed. Now I am having trouble getting undressed. My dress is over my head, caught by the keepers that prevent shoulder straps showing. Trying to undo them I get very hot. I end by having to put the dress on again and start once more. I hear the door open as I am stepping out of my pants – back-view to him.

'Não estou pronta.'

'Good,' he says, entering. I had forgotten he was deaf. He goes out. I spread the sheet on the bed and hide its scarlet. I lie down very straight. Feet together. I cover myself with the other sheet and lie motionless.

He examines my incision – his incision. It is barely discernible. That dreadful fresh scar like a large painted mouth now healed and minus its mercurochrome, half-hidden in the pubic hair.

His movements are purposeful. He is quite solemn as if listening for a far sound.

'Menstruation?'

'Not yet.'

'No?' He is surprised.

You are the only man who has ever stopped my periods, I think.

'It will return,' he said. 'I was very careful.'

That was not why I had come. 'And the pain?' I asked.

'It will pass. It sometimes happens during healing.'

I rush into my clothes when he leaves. I don't dare look at the bed.

As I go he kisses my hand. We are suddenly quite gay and glad, as if after a catastrophe, which has mercifully spared us.

He sees me to the elevator and our voices are loud and inane in the hall.

I move in a dream. Move lazily in the roaring street. He is a tiny image – the size of a reflection in a pupil. Totally secret. Small enough to recur and recur. Immobilizing.

* * *

My upbringing taught me to associate sex with love. 'And if two people love each other very, very much …' Then, by obverse reasoning? How difficult to be a parent. Is it better to tell a child the two things can be, and frequently are, quite separate? I cannot hold my parents culpable. I would probably have done the same in their place. Certainly *then*. And nine times out of ten it would have been all right.

Can one do exercises in loving? In not loving? Can one direct and teach one's passions?

Let me try.

* * *

Stuart looks at me with such wonder and love. But the small image leaps. I feel the smile of the genitals.

'We need an extra man,' he says. 'How about Henrique?'

'No.'

'No?'

'He'd fit in better with the de Mellos.'

'Then who would you suggest?'

Who? Oh, who? Somebody help me think.

* * *

That small image refuses to leave. Like a jack-in-the-box it pops up – stops me in my tracks. So much for giving myself lessons! Nothing has changed. I have not seen him again and have decided I shall not, of myself, try to see him. Our chances of meeting are rare. We met only three times before I went to

17

him professionally. But the first time had an uncanny element
to it that disturbed me even then.

Stuart was ill – too ill really to go to a dinner, yet we went.
Just before we were to dine my hostess said, 'Your husband
asked me to tell you he had to go home. He will send the car
back for you.' And then, 'Do you want to stay? I will so well
understand if you want to be with him.' But I had no car and
Stuart, I knew, would want only a quiet dark room and to be
left alone. 'No,' I said, 'I'll stay – unless it is easier for you if I
go.' It *would* have been easier, as it turned out, for we were thir-
teen at table and she was superstitious – but how could I have
known?

After dinner I sat on a sofa with him. We had been introduced just before dinner – 'How d'ye do?' 'How d'ye do.' A
small man with a red nose. The sofa held two and was placed
apart, with no chairs nearby. We were on a desert island in a sea
full of people and there we sat until protocol permitted me to
leave. I liked him. He was a surgeon. He had recently been to
my country to study our methods of deep freezing patients, so
he said. He talked of Portinari, of science, of art. We were a
long time in the hands of an inexpert hostess, marooned
together. He offered to take me home. I refused.

Stuart was better in the morning and I told him about the
party. 'He's nice,' I said, 'and bright.'

Then most unexpectedly a book of Portinari paintings
arrived with a semi-legible note. I enjoyed the book and in due
course returned it to him with a semi-legible note.

I saw him next at the Cabrals. He was with his fiancée – or
so it was rumoured. An ex-actress full of mannerisms and
affectations. I sat beside him at dinner. He described his ideal
life. 'With friends all evening. In bed all morning. Operating all
afternoon.'

Then a Sunday lunch at his house. A beautiful old colonial
house behind a wall. Deep veranda vines. Thick walls. So

tropical, so beautiful. What a wonderful world. A whole book of Debret. But I was uneasy. I found the other guests difficult. And I watched him attempting to juggle them. He served the drinks himself. Delicious food: *Vatapá. Lombo de porco.* I loved his house, disliked his party, and felt nothing about him either way.

His daughter, as a child, painted by Portinari. Wearing green shoes. The Portinari of many flecks of light against a dark ground. People – those bright flecks. Are we so bright?

* * *

The gynecologist said, 'I recommend an operation. Have you a surgeon?'

'No.'

He gave me three names.

* * *

'It's not serious,' I told Stuart afterwards, 'but it is surgery.'

He pulled a face.

'And the sooner the better.'

'Who will do it?'

'He gave me three names. I would prefer Henrique. I know him and like him. It's already a beginning.'

* * *

My appointment was at the hospital. Like a sheep on its back I greeted him, infuriated at not being allowed to see him first, dressed and on my feet.

In the small examining room he behaved as if he didn't know me. 'I find a cyst. It is best to remove it.' The telephone rang. He spoke Portuguese. He used the familiar *você.* He looked at his watch. 'At noon,' he said. 'At your house or on the corner?'

I thought of that woman and wondered about her. Was he

really going to marry her? It interested me as it would interest a novelist.

He turned to me again. He was in a hurry. 'I have no choice but to recommend surgery.' He stood up, extended his hand. 'Goodbye,' he said. Brusque.

'But wait a minute. I would like you ...'

'In that case.' He sat down again. 'I was asked only to give an opinion.'

It was decided quickly. Next week. As simple as an appointment with the hairdresser.

'Not Tuesday, I have a luncheon.'

'Wednesday I'm operating.'

'Thursday?'

'Thursday.' That's settled then.

Although he saw me in the hospital before the operation, I have no memory of it. He was not in the operating room when they rolled me in.

The nurses were in awe of him and so was I – a little. In the reversion to infancy which accompanies illness, I found him stern. His jokes at my expense did not amuse me. And there was too big a language problem. He really didn't understand English very well – certainly not the rather high-flown language of metaphor I am inclined to use under any stress. And I still spoke a kind of child's Portuguese.

He took to entering my room in a small explosion of bad English that so confused me I frequently forgot to say the things I had been planning for hours.

I found myself night after night opening my eyes and seeing him standing by my bed. 'I have a very sick patient in the hospital and I just looked in to see you on my way.'

The night superintendent of nurses said, 'He certainly looks after *you*.'

'Nonsense, he has another patient here who is very sick and he ...'

'He has no other patients here.' Her pretty blue eyes grew round and full of a sudden comprehension. She put her cupped hand over her mouth in alarm.

'*Don't* tell him I told you. *Please!*'

'Perhaps not on this floor,' I said.

'Not on this floor, not on *any* floor. You're the *only* patient he has anywhere in the building.'

As related, this seems to have more significance than it had then. I remember it now. Then it was unimportant. I don't even recall trying to figure out his reasons for coming. Perhaps I was very sick. But I don't think I felt any undue concern over my condition. It was all just part of the slightly surreal life of illness.

* * *

He discharged me from hospital and said he would see me in a month.

It was wonderful to be home. The house was quiet and very beautiful. A slightly hushed staff greeted me. They were self-conscious seeing me in my dressing gown walking on the terrace in the sun – slowly, peacefully. I was very happy. There were no pressures on me. The household ran smoothly. For a few days I even had a child. The laundress's daughter attached herself to me – a soft little cross-eyed girl who wore a perfume that smelled slightly of urine. We drew together and she was very patient with my Portuguese. Quite wonderfully she drew fingers like ribbons growing out from arms. The weather was hot. Day after day of sun. The mountains still as a painting. A green world.

The days passed smoothly, peacefully. Stuart came and went. Friends dropped in for coffee. The house was filled with flowers. I read and I drew.

At month's end Henrique paid a house call. He examined his 'signature', as he called it. Said I would carry it with me for life.

Proclaimed me *'ótimo'*. Said yes, of course I could swim and anything else I liked.

'Golf,' he suggested.

'I don't golf.'

'Bom,' he said. He told me he was going to his *fazenda* for two weeks, gave me the name of his partner in case I needed a surgeon in his absence.

'I dismiss you,' he said. 'You are no longer my patient.'

He took my hand, leaned towards me. I was in turmoil.

'Kiss me.'

I turned my face away.

'As you wish,' he said. He kissed my hand. *'Boa tarde.'*

I rang for a servant to see him out.

And I could not bear it.

* * *

'What did he say?' Stuart asked, business-like, on his return. 'Have you passed muster?'

I nodded. 'He said I can swim. Play golf!'

'Did he say we could make love?' Stuart said. 'Now?'

* * *

Then the pains began. Not bad pains – but bad enough to waken me and keep me awake. Bad enough to make me limp slightly. At the end of the week, bad enough to make me feel worn out and wretched.

'Get in touch with the other surgeon,' my husband said, but I preferred to wait. It was an unreasonable kind of loyalty. If something was the matter – and I had by now begun to think there was – I would sooner Henrique's partner was not the one to discover it.

The morning he was due back I phoned. His servant could not understand me or I her. At noon I tried again. Only with the greatest difficulty did I reach him then. He arrived on the phone in an explosion of Portuguese. *'É um prazer falar com você. Como vai, como vai?'*

'Não muito bem.'

'Muito bem? Ótimo!'

'Não, não – eu disse não muito bem.' I was close to tears. The pain had gone on too long.

The appointment, this time, was in his consulting room.

* * *

The decision to lose one's virginity is very different from the decision to cuckold one's husband. In the first instance one has only oneself to consider, which alters the nature of the decision. Looking back I am surprised to find the first decision was not made in the height of passion. *That* I had withstood. I made a deliberate intellectual choice. 'Next time,' I had said to myself. Meaning it.

This comforts me a bit for I find it difficult to believe that intellectually I could decide to cuckold my husband.

But I wanted to see him. I scanned the parties ahead, wondering. Might he possibly be at dinner at the de L's on the 12th? I found myself on the night of the 12th taking special pains with my appearance. And it was then, looking at myself in the mirror, that I made a decision: *I will do nothing to further the relationship.*

Only as we went into the dining room, when I realized for certain that he was not there, did I know how much I had counted on seeing him. The evening became insufferable. The enchanting young man beside me had to work far too hard. He had, indeed, got out his drag nets. Young man, young man, I am sorry, but I am not here.

* * *

Now a new panic develops. My physician has insisted I see Henrique again. A urinary problem. I postpone phoning. In two days, God be thanked, my symptoms have lessened. I tell Stuart. He says the GP would not have asked me to go without a reason. We argue mildly and I am suddenly overcome with the need to tell him what he is doing. But I say nothing. Instead, I phone the physician.

'My symptoms have gone. It is not worth bothering Henrique now,' I say firmly.

He is obdurate. But still I do not make an appointment.

'Have you phoned Henrique?' asks my husband.

'No.'

'Why not?' He is slightly irritated.

Why not have a gynecological examination by a man...!

We are dressing to go out. Perversely, knowing I cannot see him tonight, I allow myself the complicated luxury of dressing for him.

'Why don't you phone him now?'

'He'll be having dinner.'

'Oh, God!' says my husband.

I don't use the upstairs phone. I go downstairs, dial as if guilty, my hands trembling. The smell of my perfume is strong on the air.

He answers. Is jovial. The appointment is made. For Thursday. Tonight is Tuesday. 'At three – no, wait a minute. At four-thirty.'

'Yes,' I say but I am beside myself. I cannot possibly go through with it. If he were to examine me I would have to make a confession I do not intend to make. I am a fool to have agreed to the appointment. Tomorrow I will call and cancel it. Yet how can I? How do I explain myself to the physician? To Stuart? 'I am so infatuated that the mere thought ...'

Let me pretend to feel nothing. Nothing. Strange word, nothing. But now, of course, I am overwhelmed by him. He is with me every minute. I fling myself at life with a kind of madness.

'I will do nothing to further the relationship,' I had said. And what have I done?

Stop thinking. Turn him off like a light. Many years ago my older half-sister had astonished me by saying, 'I shall destroy my love for my son. It has only become destructive to him, so I shall destroy it.'

'But how?' I was genuinely curious.

'I shall turn it off as one turns off a light.'

'Turn it *off?*'

Turn it off, then.

* * *

There are times when I am semi-detached, only to be obsessed again. Moments when I am so plunged in the implications of it all that I wonder Stuart has not noticed.

Absurd how I long to say, 'Help me, Stuart. You know I love you. Our life together is good. We have worked through to this – not without difficulty for us both. Help me, now. Help save us.'

Why must I make so much of everything? Why must an infatuation of very short duration already assume such giant proportions, such earth-shaking dimensions?

If I could say to Stuart, 'It is nothing. It will pass.' But if it doesn't pass? If it doesn't?

* * *

The afternoon has arrived. Good God, how many times have I washed? I wear a blouse and skirt. I had my hair done this morning and it is hideous. Hideous. Then, all the better.

A male nurse greets me. There is a patient inside. I can hear her voice.

If someone were to stand me on my feet, my skeleton would not support me. I would fall, a pile of clothing and flesh, to the floor.

Think of something else.

The door opens. I don't look up. Out of the corner of my eye I see a woman pass. He is framed in the lighted door. He is wearing his white coat – arms bare to the elbows.

'*Boa tarde.*'

'Hello.'

'*Momentinho.*' I hear the water running in the far room as he washes.

I am calmer already.

'Tea?' he says. And we have tea together in his beautiful baroque room. But it is not safe. The stillness of danger is here. I cannot keep my body still enough. Nor my mind. With all my might.

So much of our conversation is misunderstanding. Often I cannot understand him in either language – or he me. He is full of formal compliments which I disregard. And then I press him to get on with the examination. I must leave soon. We are due out at seven.

He leads me to the little red bed. And leaves me. I take off my clothing and lie, so I imagine, like a dead virgin in my slip and pearls on the red bed, my head on the green pillow. The sheet comes only to my waist.

When he returns his manner changes. He is quite open.

'You look lovely,' he says. 'The green looks wonderful under your hair.' And quite frankly he stares, admiring.

Is the ear of the male nurse pressed against the door?

'Cough,' he says and he palpates my incision. 'Cough,' he says again. 'Cough.' I cough and cough.

'Philipe was afraid part of your bladder was caught in the incision. But it's not.' He kissed the back of my hand. Then its palm.

He got up. There was only a slatted wall between the two rooms. He withdrew behind the slats while I dressed.

'So *that* was why he insisted I come to you. I didn't want to, you know.'

'Which only shows that Philipe is my very good friend and you are not.'

'Yes?'

There is an enormous relief in me. I was not forced into any confession. For the moment I am safe.

He catches my hand and perhaps because I am so filled with relief I am off guard. His next remark falls like a hammer on my heart.

'I was very pleased when we met – very happy to have met you. You knew that, didn't you? You remember the occasion. And I was very angry when you came to me as a patient. Very angry indeed. You put me in an impossible position. I was in love with you. Surely you knew. Yet you asked me to operate. For a surgeon to cut into the flesh of someone he loves ...'

I could hardly bear what he said. I had not known. Why had I not? Had I ignored the signs? But what signs were there – the loaned book? the invitation to luncheon? Surely not.

* * *

I drove home by the sea, the beautiful warm extravagant night soft on my skin. A tremendous fatigue and a great slow sadness filled me. A kind of ultimate melancholy – as if I had suddenly learned the meaning and the terrible poignancy of 'forever'.

Our house glowed in the darkness. All its windows as if lighted by candles. Stuart was already home. I went into his study. He was not there. I went upstairs, calling his name.

He was in bed reading. He looked up, glad to see me.

'Have you seen the surgeon?'

I sat on the side of his bed. 'Yes.' He pulled me to him.

'What did he have to say?'

'Apparently Philipe wanted to know if my bladder was caught in the incision. It isn't.'

'Is that all he told you?'

'Yes.'

'What else happened today?'

'Nothing much. And you?'

'Just a series of small annoyances.'

'We must dress, I suppose.' I was so tired. So filled with despair. 'Must we really go?'

'You'll enjoy it when you get there.'

I was astonished to find I looked quite nice as we left – quite Brazilian. In black, with mink and pearls.

I pitched myself into a group where I had to speak Portuguese, where my total concentration was needed. And then I saw his partner. 'Every doctor in town is here tonight,' he said. 'A medical convention.' He laughed. I doubted Henrique's presence. I simply didn't feel it.

But suddenly, as if a torch were ignited, he was beside me, looking all crossed sticks. Quite fierce.

* * *

That night I had a snake dream. The first of my life. Common though they are said to be, I had not had one before. Our driver was holding a large one. Someone I do not remember had a small black one. An immense venomous one miraculously pushed through the tightly woven Caucasian carpet. I was delighted. Awakened laughing.

'What's so funny?' Stuart asked.

'A dream.'

We leave by car for Lages. I am glad to be away. Glad of the distractions of new things. But – I am not distracted. I am a sleeping top.

I don't understand why things have moved so fast. Why already I suffer such pain. It all seems back to front like the New Guineans' introduction to transportation: first the plane, then the truck, then the horse. For me the plane has come long before the horse.

In our hotel room twin beds. On a dressing table opposite
are two vases of flowers. In the morning all the flowers in 'my'
vase are dead. Stuart's are fresh as ever.

Before breakfast I picked a pomegranate from its tree and
ate it. Found a strange pleasure as the clear red crystals broke
into bitter-sweet juice and left only savourless pithy seeds. As if
I were acting out the entire course of love.

* * *

During the night I come to the overwhelming realization that I
cannot hurt Stuart. How strange this delicate balance between
us. He is already compensating for my withdrawal – a withdrawal I swear he cannot consciously feel. There is a certain
panic in his love. A pressing towards me, a greater enfolding of
me in his heart. In the night he wakened me with cries of terror.
Were his dreams telling him what I wasn't? I renounced Henrique at that moment and as I did so realized that with that
decision I had left my youth behind and I wept at this, the most
terrible renunciation of all.

* * *

Tuesday he called. 'Come to tea. I must talk to you.'

After some thought I accepted. It is playing with fire, but I
lead from strength, or so I thought. I must work out with him
what I should do if I were to need a surgeon. And, too – out of
vanity, I fear – I would like him to know that I had no idea he
was in love with me when I asked him to be my surgeon. Well,
we shall see if it *was* strength!

Miraculously I slipped into a kind of emotional side street.
Quite tranquil there. The furious physical desire abated. Was it
because of a conversation with his partner's wife?

'Do you know Henrique?' she asked, out of the blue.

'Of course. He operated on me.' Why did she ask?

'Don't you find him a very lonely person?'

'I don't know. What's happened to the woman he was going to marry?'

'There have been a succession of women. The first was one of the most attractive Brazilians I have ever met. He had an affair with her and was on the point of getting a divorce to marry her when she made a fatal mistake. She told him that his wife was having an affair. So then he did a thing of great character. He divorced his wife and didn't marry his mistress.'

I was bewildered by this. 'But why did he divorce his wife?'

'Because she was having an affair.'

'But ...'

'I know. It seems absurd. But they're *Brazilians*.'

I suddenly felt quite sick and very tired. I wanted to go to the sea and let a great wave break over me.

* * *

On Tuesday I shall see him. I shall say ... but there seems almost no need to say anything now. It no longer matters that he know that I didn't know, etc., etc.

Perhaps I am through this. Safe out the other side. And no one hurt.

* * *

Tuesday. Portuguese lesson rather depressing. I have hit a plateau. Will I ever master the subjunctives, which are used in the most colloquial of conversations by quite uneducated people? An extraordinary language. My *professora* was moody and abstracted. She must be in love. Perhaps everybody is – the heat keeping us all at fever pitch.

There is time to spare between my lesson and tea with Henrique. I look for material for a new dress and suddenly I can barely walk with tension. Going up to his office I lean against the wall of the elevator, put the back of my wrist against my forehead, catch myself doing it and am half amused.

I am early. I hear through the door the harsh voices of Brazilian women. His male nurse is not there. I start to leave but the waiting room fills – an older woman and a younger, possibly her daughter, and Henrique. He sees the women to the door and we are together in the consulting room.

He takes my hands. 'Your hands are wet.'

'The result of a wish I made as a child. And the gods were kind.'

'I love you.'

'This is not love.'

'What is love then?'

'I don't know.'

'Isn't this a part of love?'

'Perhaps yes.'

'I miss you so much. I ...'

'Don't.'

'There are tears in your eyes.'

'You're wrong. It's my hands, not my eyes that are wet.'

But he is right. What am I doing sitting crying?

He goes back to the days of the hospital. 'I had to be so strict with myself. I think I was sometimes almost rude to you.'

'Almost!'

'You noticed?'

'It would have been hard to miss.'

'Forgive me.'

There is no pleasure in this. I survey the vast desert of my life as he talks.

I get up. 'Goodbye.'

'When can I see you?'

'You can't.'

'When can I phone?'

'You can't.'

'Why be strong when it is so sweet to be weak?'

I give no answer.

'Look at me. I am going to my *fazenda* on Thursday. I am coming back on Monday.'

I am grateful to know that from now until Monday I cannot meet him or hear from him. 'I shall phone you Tuesday.'

'No.'

'Then meet me here.'

I get up. He tries to kiss me but when I turn my mouth away he lets me go.

'Goodbye.'

'Don't say that.'

'*Até logo*, then.'

'Better.'

He opens the door to his waiting room and I am faced by two young men. I am caught completely off guard. I had thought we were alone, the office empty. I turn back. Drop my keys.

We start again. He sees me to the elevator. 'All my love.'

I press the button for the ground floor and the elevator goes up.

* * *

On Monday at the concert he passes me during intermission. He is with the 'actress' and walks almost right through me.

'There's Henrique,' Stuart says and makes an attempt to catch him. The crowd closes like a door between them. Momentarily I am upside down and glad of its support and its screen.

* * *

'We must have him to dinner,' Stuart says. 'Soon.'

I don't answer. Henrique at our long table among the silver and glass.

'Let's make a list. The de Mellos, Henrique ...'

I cut him short. 'A reception,' I say.

Stuart brushes the idea aside with his arm as if it were an object. 'The de Mellos, Henrique, and how about that architect and …' And. And. And. The list is made. The date chosen.

* * *

That night as if I had a rigour, I shook and shook. Stuart so tender, so inarticulate, so loving.

'I think you should see a doctor,' he says.

'It is nothing. It will pass.' But I want to say, 'Fight for me. Please, please fight for me. I need your help.'

* * *

The morning of the dinner, the papers announce the death of two prominent politicians. We must cancel our dinner. The government is in mourning. But the pre-party flowers have been ordered ahead. A boy walks slowly up the long drive, an enormous *cesta* on his head. Flowers like birds. My heart pounds. From Henrique? I reach for the card. No. And later, dozens of red roses. Surely from Henrique. No, once more.

Is he stingy? I play with the idea. Perhaps he is. All this love and no celebration of it in presents. He said he would send me Bandeira but he has not. He says he is waiting for a new edition. I decide he *is* stingy and comfort myself.

I expect him to phone – *saudades*. But no.

So?

And then his partner's wife phones. 'Did you hear about Henrique?'

I don't want to talk to her about him. Don't like her gossipy tongue. Don't trust her.

'No,' I say, sharply perhaps.

'Well, he's dead.'

'But he was coming to dinner with us,' I say inanely as if that changed things.

'He won't be now. He was on the same plane as the ministers. They were all killed.' Her voice broke suddenly. 'Isn't it awful!'

I put the phone back in its cradle with intense concentration.

Dead? Henrique? It cannot be true.

The phone rings again. Henrique, I think. But it's Stuart. His voice is grave.

'I have sad, bad news. About Henrique,' he says. 'I am coming right home.'

(1999)

The Sky Tree

The King and Queen were old. They had ruled their country wisely and well for many years. No one had ever gone hungry in Ure for the granaries were always full. Traders came from the four corners of the world to buy crystallized fruits for which the country was famous. When royalty from other kingdoms wanted jewels for their crowns, or rings for their fingers, they sent messengers to Ure because its rubies were as red as pigeon's blood and its sapphires as blue as the sea.

One day the Queen and King – Meera and Galaad to their friends – were strolling slowly through the Palace grounds with Treece, their only son. The Queen (who walked with a slight limp) said, 'I *would* so like see the Wizard again.' She inclined her head slightly towards the King to hear his reply. 'So would I! So would I!' said the King.

'The Wizard?' Treece was suddenly interested. 'What Wizard?'

'Have we never told you?' asked his mother vaguely.

'Tell me now,' said Treece. 'Please tell me now.'

The Queen and the King exchanged glances, and then the Queen began. 'A long time ago, before my father died and you were born, Ure was a landlocked kingdom. Travel was not as common then as it is today and the people of Ure had never seen the sea.'

'They didn't believe in it, either,' the King laughed.

'Didn't believe in the sea!' Treece exclaimed.

'For some people, if they have never seen a thing, it's hard for them to believe in it. Unless it is love,' he said dreamily. 'Or rage, perhaps.'

'… more importantly, the lands bordering the Eastern Sea belonged to a wicked Wizard,' the Queen continued, picking up where she had been interrupted. 'Your father knew him well.'

'Too well,' the King said. 'He turned me into a goatherd.'

'But I thought you *were* a goatherd – when you were a boy, I mean.'

'Quite right, Treece,' the King replied. 'The first time, I was a goatherd by birth and occupation. The second time, I was a goatherd by magic – black magic. The Wizard cast a spell upon me. Then, later still, after your mother and I were married, we met the Wizard again, face to face. And we fought.'

'Fought!' said Treece. 'But we don't fight in Ure.'

'Your father was very brave,' the Queen said, ignoring his remark.

'And your mother was very clever,' added the King proudly. 'It was a terrible fight. He used his Magic Blasting Rod.'

'Did you kill him?' asked Treece.

'In a kind of a way,' said his mother. 'We forced him into the sea and –'

'Did he drown?' asked Treece. 'No, he couldn't have drowned, for you want to see him again. Oh, do go on!'

'What we *didn't* know,' continued the King, 'was that the Wizard, too, was under a spell, and once in sea water he was no longer a wicked Wizard with a Blasting Rod, but a beautiful young man – as bright as the sun. The sea, you understand, can break such spells.'

'Silvery and golden,' said the Queen. 'I should love to see him again. I think of him all the time.'

'Where is he now?' Treece was practical as well as interested.

'That's just it,' said the Queen and King together. 'We don't know. You see, he said goodbye and then … he vanished. Into thin air.'

'He couldn't just vanish!' said Treece. 'It isn't possible.'

———

'Many things are not possible,' said the King, 'and yet ...' He shrugged. 'It is not possible for a goatherd to marry a Princess. But it happened. It is not possible for a person to vanish into thin air. But the Wizard did. Before our eyes. Like that.' The King snapped his fingers.

'Not before telling us that he would come back,' the Queen said. 'But he never has.'

'Then you must search the Kingdom for him,' Treece said.

'Oh, he's not in Ure,' his father replied. 'Not anywhere here. You see, he went home.'

* * *

'What do you think about Treece?' the King asked, when he and Queen were alone together. 'Do you think he can rule the Kingdom when we are gone?'

'I think he would make a *fine* ruler. He's a good boy. Honest and kind. Considerate too.'

'But is he strong?' asked the King. 'And brave? Could he face uncertainty and danger?'

'If the occasion arose, I am sure he could. He has never had a chance to prove himself because we have had no wars during our reign.' She looked at the King. 'You don't foresee danger, do you?'

'No, no, no. Of course not. It is just that a good ruler must be able ...' the King began, but he could see the Queen was not listening.

'I really *would* like to see the Wizard again,' she said. 'He *did* say he'd come back. Didn't he?'

'I'm not sure,' said her husband. 'I thought he said we would meet again.'

'There you are!' The Queen was mildly triumphant. 'How could we see him if he didn't come back?'

'*We* might go to *him*,' said the King.

The Queen shook her head sadly. 'But if we don't know

where he is, where would we go?'

The King was silent. Thinking. 'I have an idea,' he said at last. 'Let us talk to Erland and Corille and see what they remember.'

Corille and Erland had also known the Wizard well – too well. He had cast a spell upon both of them that had turned them into goats! That was many years ago when the Queen was Princess Meera and the King was a young goatherd.

Corille and Erland had been with them later on that extraordinary day when they had forced the wicked Wizard into the sea. They had been there, too, when he had emerged dripping – silvery and golden – no longer a wicked Wizard but a being such as they had never before seen or imagined. A being they could never forget.

'He did say he would come back, didn't he?' Meera was certain Corille and Erland would agree.

But neither one of them could remember.

'Didn't he say something about going home?' Erland asked.

They were all quiet, trying to remember. He was so silvery and golden, so full of laughter and light. So tall. Different entirely from any of them. They longed to see him, each one of them. But they did not know how to begin to look.

'What about your Fairy Godmother?' Corille asked Meera, suddenly. 'Wouldn't she help? She did once.'

'My Fairy Godmother!' Meera exclaimed. 'I had almost forgotten about her. She only ever came when I needed her very badly, and it's years since I've needed anything at all. Why, I don't know where she is or even how to find her.'

'Why don't you just call her, the way you did before?' Corille suggested.

* * *

And so Queen Meera called. Out loud she called. She called every day for a week. Nothing happened. She called every day for a month. And still nothing happened.

'What do you think I should do now?' she asked Galaad.

'We must just go on believing she will come,' he said.

One night when they were sitting on their balcony looking at the stars, the King – telescope to eye – said, 'There's a most extraordinary object in the sky. Look!' and he handed the telescope to the Queen.

'A bar,' said the Queen. 'A pearly bar.'

As they watched, it rushed towards them at a remarkable speed. Then, immediately overhead, it stopped, and began a slow descent until its lower end came to rest on the railing of their balcony – a great pearly bar reaching from the stars. It gave off an astonishing light.

And who should come down it, as if it were a flight of stairs, but the Fairy Godmother herself, glittering like diamonds.

'You look as if you are made of fire,' the Queen said, her face shining with pleasure.

'Fairies are made of fire,' the Godmother answered.

'Fiery Godmother,' said the King, laughing at his own joke, but at the same time understanding something he had not understood before.

'You needed me,' the Fairy Godmother said, 'so I came. How can I help you?'

'We would like to find the Wizard,' the Queen said.

'Ah-h-h-h!' said the Fairy Godmother. 'There are many who would like to find him.'

'And we don't know where to look,' said the King.

'Where have you looked?' the Fairy Godmother asked.

'Well, actually, nowhere – yet,' said the King. 'You see, he said he had to go home, and we don't know where home is.'

'It is – everywhere,' said the Fairy Godmother, and she waved her wand in a great circle which took in all of heaven and earth. 'You must search,' she said. 'Land, sea and air.'

'We are old,' said the Queen. 'Searching is no longer as easy as when we were young.'

'But finding is sometimes easier.' The Fairy Godmother placed her small shining foot on the bottom of the pearly bar which, like an escalator, took her up, up and out of sight before they could open their mouths even to say goodbye.

* * *

'Finding is sometimes easier,' said the King and the Queen over and over again in the weeks that followed. Not that it was proving so for them

To begin with, because they themselves could no longer travel, they had to call upon the realm's Searchers – men and women with eyes as sharp as hawks' and noses and ears as keen as dogs'. The Searchers were specially trained to find missing objects, missing pets and missing persons. They were not police. Ure had no need for police, but it did need Searchers. They had found many things, some that were deeply hidden, like memories and dreams, to say nothing of rings dropped down wells, cats stuck in trees, and people who had taken the wrong road home in the dark.

The King and Queen knew that if the Wizard were anywhere in the Kingdom, or even in the neighbouring lands, the Searchers would find him.

The first report of a sighting was in the capital of Ure itself. The Searchers had not actually seen the Wizard, but someone answering to that description had been seen – and not long ago. And not far from the Palace grounds, either. No one could say exactly when, or exactly where. But a tall man had been sighted, very tall – all silvery and golden.

After that, not a day went by but a new account of the Wizard reached them from somewhere. He had been seen in the high mountain passes. Or helping the workers pick fruit in the orchards. Once he had been seen walking on the waves. And everyone who had seen him claimed to have felt better afterwards. But none could say where he was now, where he had come from, why he stayed for so short a time among them, or why, sometimes, he walked away, or just vanished, leaving the people shaking their heads with wonder.

Each day the Searchers sent their reports to the Palace. And now everyone in the Kingdom was on the alert for the Wizard, whom they knew to be there among them, moving like summer lightning – bright, beautiful, but always beyond reach.

It was clear to the King and Queen that the Searchers had seen him over and over again. But like a fish that no net could hold, he was found only to be lost again – not from memory, of course, but from *there*, wherever it was he had been seen.

So the King and Queen recalled the Searchers to the Palace and thanked them and sent them back to searching once again for all the objects, pets and people that had disappeared during the time they had been looking for the Wizard.

* * *

'Did you find the Wizard?' asked the Fairy Godmother, awash with starlight as she came once again at the Queen's call.

'Yes and no,' said the Queen. And she told the Fairy Godmother the whole story, which of course, she already knew.

'You have searched the land and the sea,' said the Godmother. 'The only place left is the air.'

The King, the Queen, and the Fairy Godmother were together on the balcony. How brilliantly the night stars shone! The constellation Schooner was like a great ship of lights above them. The King and the Queen were craning their necks in wonder when, in an unexpected rush of air, they found themselves on board that pearly bar and rising high into the sky. Incomparably high.

Below, their Palace with its courtyards and banquet rooms seemed nothing more than a cluster of bright dots, while the earth itself, pricked with the lights of Ure and Ure's neighbouring kingdoms, might have been the night sky as they had seen it many times from their balcony.

How wonderful this ascent into the night, with shooting stars glowing and disappearing all around them. And was it their eyesight or the effect of the starlight that made them young again? When the Queen looked at the King he seemed hardly more than a boy. And when the King looked at the Queen, he saw the black-haired Princess he had fallen in love with when he was a goatherd.

The pearly bar slowed and came to a stop in a world of rainbows. Free of the air of earth, colours were different. To their surprise, the Fairy Godmother was purest violet. Beside her was another being, as beautiful as she, who was deepest indigo; and next to her a blue, then a green and a yellow and an orange and a red. And beyond them were ranks and ranks of other beings – some multicoloured, and some almost transparent, like crystal – who made way for a stream of perfect smaller beings, as bright as fireflies, who accompanied the Queen of Faerie. She was surely the most beautiful person in all the heavens, or wherever they were in this realm of air. Great crowds assembled around her in rainbow formation when she sat on a cushion of cloud and beckoned the King and Queen to sit beside her.

She offered them food unknown on earth, and delicious drinks out of goblets that reflected all the colours of the rainbow and, as they ate, the fairies sang songs sweeter than anything heard in Ure, in keys that only Faerie knew. And when the dancing began, the King and the Queen found that their feet danced as fast as fairies' feet.

'Guests at my court,' said the Queen of Faerie, when the dancing ended, 'always receive a gift. I grant their heart's desire.'

The King and the Queen spoke as one. 'Our heart's desire is to find the Wizard.'

'One heart's desire for two people!' said the Queen of Faerie. 'Remarkable. In that case, you may have a lesser wish, as well.'

The King and Queen hadn't thought of lesser wishes, so strong was their desire to see the Wizard.

'What about Corille and Erland?' Galaad suggested, and Meera agreed.

In a flash Corille and Erland appeared, rubbing their eyes as if they had just wakened, looking about them in wonder. And they, too, were young, just as they had been when they first met Meera and Galaad.

The Queen of Faerie offered refreshments, and told them that if they could name it, she would give them each their heart's desire.

'My heart's desire?' said Corille. 'Oh-h-h ... happiness. Eternal happiness,' and she held out her hand to Erland.

And Erland, in his turn, seeing Corille as beautiful as she had ever been, said his heart's desire was that he and Corille should remain together until the end of time.

* * *

Overhead, an enormous chandelier filled the night sky – or so it appeared. It was made of stars and stars and more stars. And yet it was a tree. Astonished by its height, Meera and Galaad and Corille and Erland surveyed it. It was as if they were lying on their backs in Ure and looking up into the branches of the tallest tree in the land, one that was covered with thousands of lights.

'The Sky Tree,' said the Queen of Faerie, and a shiver went through them at the name. 'It leads to the Wizard.'

Its many branches and glittering lights were bewildering, and as they stared into what must surely have been infinity, they felt like mere dots in all that space.

'The Sky Tree leads to the Wizard?' Meera asked, in a small voice. 'It looks awfully difficult.'

'Oh, it is difficult,' said the Queen of Faerie. 'But it's not impossible.'

'What should we take with us?' asked Corille, troubled by the thought of the climb.

'That you will have to decide for yourselves,' said the Queen of Faerie. 'I can't even advise you, for you are leaving my realm and going to one about which I know little.'

'I shan't take anything,' said Meera. 'Only the clothes I have on.'

'We'll need our hands free for climbing,' Galaad said. And as they removed their crowns and jewels they saw that, in this realm of Faerie, the most precious stones from Ure looked like nothing more than coloured glass, and its gold was without lustre.

'You can leave your jewels, if you like,' said Corille, 'but I'm going to take my necklace and my ring. They're light. And they're pretty. And I love them.'

As they said goodbye to the Queen of Faerie, all the beautiful creatures of her court assembled to see them leave, for it was not often that anyone dared to climb the Sky Tree.

'You are going where I am no longer of any help,' Meera's Fairy Godmother said, and shed a tear. 'I shall not even be able to hear you if you call.'

Galaad looked at Meera. 'You first,' he said, remembering how well she had climbed trees when she was young. 'I'll be right behind you.'

Meera jumped, grabbed the lowest branch of the Sky Tree, and swung herself up.

The climbing was easy at first, for they were young and nimble and strong. Corille and Erland were especially happy, remembering the last time all four of them had been together on the adventure which had ended with their meeting the Wizard face to face. And now here they were on a greater adventure still, climbing the Sky Tree which, they were told, would lead them to the Wizard once again.

Seen from the Land of Faerie, the stars that formed the tree had appeared very close together, but now those same stars were separated by great airy spaces through which the climbers had to swing like trapeze artists. 'Don't look down,' said Corille, who just had, and whose head was spinning. 'Could we stop? I'm starving. Did anyone bring food?'

'I've found a perfect place to rest,' said Meera from above. And she had. It was a kind of a nest made from small soft stars which glowed and gave off a comfortable warmth.

Nearby, bright fruits grew on silver vines. Corille picked one and held it in her hand. It gave off a faint light and fragrance. They all looked at it a long time. They wondered if it was poison. Then Corille, who was hungriest, took a tiny bite. 'Mmm-mm!' she said. 'Delicious! Have some.' The smallest bite made them feel they had eaten an entire meal.

* * *

Refreshed, they began the climb again. The Sky Tree was just like a ordinary tree except for its size and the fact that its branches shone, and its leaves, when touched, fell in a shower of sparks only to grow again in burst of light.

At first there had been no birds in the branches, but suddenly the leaves were full of them – birds of all kinds – invisible in the darkness but whistling and singing and talking. One splendid parrot kept repeating, 'Right this way. Right this way,' as he led them from the night through which they had been climbing into a land, sunny and beautiful with rushing streams and natural fountains gushing out of grassy knolls.

'How beautiful!' Corille cried, happy at the sight of green fields again. 'And look – people! Laughing and dancing!'

In no time at all Meera, Galaad, Corille and Erland were dancing too. Such steps they danced, such intricate, fast steps.

'It's wonderful!' said Meera as she and Galaad ran dripping

from the stream. But suddenly, she was reminded of how she and Galaad had run dripping from the sea with the Wizard between them, and that memory, although sweet, was like a pain in her heart. 'Galaad, we must go,' she said. 'We must find the Wizard.'

'Perhaps he's here,' said Corille, who did not want to leave.

Meera shook her head. 'He's not here. I feel sure of it.' And Galaad agreed.

So they began once again on their climb to find the Wizard.

Because they had grown accustomed to daylight, the night world, beautiful though it was, felt strange to them.

Everything was more difficult now. They were clumsy and slow. Even Meera had trouble finding a handhold, and Galaad had barely the strength to pull himself up.

Then from the darkness below Corille called, 'Help! Oh, help! I – I'm stuck.'

Erland, first to reach her, found her necklace was entangled in a thicket of glittering twigs. 'It won't take a minute,' he said, for it looked simple. But it was not.

'I can't *move*,' Corille said.

Galaad joined them. It was as if the twigs were alive, for no matter what they did to untangle the necklace, the twigs tangled it again. 'You'll have to take it off,' Galaad said, finally. 'We'll disentangle it when you're free.' Corille undid the clasp, and Erland tried again. But nothing they did to work it loose had any effect. It just got more and more tangled. Finally Corille, sad because she loved her necklace, decided she must leave it behind.

Great birds moved in the branches overhead – dark birds. Their feathers shone like jet. The stars of the Sky Tree dimmed and went out. One by one.

'This way, this way,' croaked the birds, and they cackled with terrible laughter as they led the climbers into a darkness so black that they could no longer see each other.

'I'm frightened here,' said Corille. 'I want to go back to that beautiful place where everyone was happy.'

Erland, whose only wish was to be with Corille, wherever she was, agreed.

But Meera and Galaad said they must find the Wizard.

'Oh, do come with us,' Corille pleaded. 'It was lovely there and we've all been friends for so long and I know we'd be happy.'

But Meera and Galaad had to go on.

And so the couples parted. And as Corille and Erland began their descent, Meera and Galaad struggled upwards again through what was now a pitch-black night, with only the taunting cackles of the black birds as their guide. 'I must say I'm a bit frightened myself,' said Meera.

'We'll be all right,' Galaad replied. 'We've got each other. And whether we like them or not, we've got the birds.'

'This way. This way,' the feathered creatures croaked. 'This way.'

Meera began to tire. 'Galaad, we must stop. I can't go any further. I can't see to climb. I'm hungry and thirsty and tired.'

But the only answer was the terrible cackle of the black birds' laughter, followed by silence. The most enormous total silence.

'Galaad!' Meera called, suddenly terrified. 'Galaad, where are you? Oh, Galaad!' How could he have left her without any warning or word of goodbye? If he had fallen, surely he would have cried out and she would have heard him. But if he were anywhere near he would have answered.

'I'm all alone,' Meera said to herself, unbelieving. She crouched on a narrow branch – neither comfortable nor safe. For support, she clung to a smaller branch above her head. If she lost her balance for even a second she would fall through that endless all-surrounding night – the night in which she had lost Galaad. She could see nothing. Hear nothing. 'Oh,

Galaad,' she cried, 'where can you be? How could we have
become separated like this?'

Fingers touched her hand. For a moment she thought
Galaad had returned. But almost immediately she knew that it
was not Galaad. Whoever it was, was uncurling her fingers one
by one. Loosening her grip on the branch. 'No!' she called out
in panic. 'No! Go away! Please!' But as quickly as she gripped
the branch afresh, those hidden fingers began again, uncurling
her fingers one by one. And they were strong – stronger than
she was.

* * *

Galaad didn't know what had happened. One moment he had
been climbing in the dark with Meera, following the voices that
called, 'This way, this way,' and the next he was all alone in a
pitch-dark night, unable to see or hear anything at all. Worst of
all he had lost Meera. 'Meera,' he called. 'Meera!' Not even an
echo answered.

Only a minute before she had been talking to him. Now she
had gone. The thought that she might have slipped and fallen
filled his heart with dread. He called her again, 'Meeeera!'

At that moment something soft was placed over his mouth.
How could he reach Meera if he could no longer call to find out
where she was? And if he could not find her.... The thought
was unbearable. He felt himself wrapped round and round
with ropes, legs bound together, arms tied to his sides. If Meera
should call him now, he would be unable to answer or move. He
waited for something more to happen. Perhaps they would take
him away, whoever they were. But having wrapped him up like
a mummy, they seemed to have disappeared and left him alone
in the dark and terrible silence.

He had no idea how long he had hung there gagged and
helpless before he heard, quite clearly, the words the Wizard
had spoken by the sea, all those years ago, 'We shall meet

again.' The voice was nearby, almost inside him.

He concentrated with all his power on the memory of that silver and golden figure, and listened intently to hear what else he might say. And as he visualized the Wizard, a sprinkling of notes sounded in the silent night. At the same time the darkness filled with millions of grains of light, so tiny and so many – golden kernels pouring from a cornucopia – that they created a great luminous field.

Within it, like a body on fire, in a suit of lights, stood the Wizard.

* * *

A Wizard, of course, has the power to find any person who searches for him. It is almost as if that person is made of iron filings which the Wizard's magnet can attract.

And because Galaad had looked so hard for the Wizard, the Wizard found Galaad. In all that darkness, in all that silence, the Wizard found Galaad.

* * *

Meanwhile, back in Ure, the King and the Queen were missing.

Treece was alarmed and puzzled. They had never disappeared before, and on those rare occasions when they had had to go away, they had always told him ahead of time, and formally handed over their responsibilities in the presence of the Lord Chamberlain. This time they had just vanished.

When the Attendants in the Royal Bedchamber said they had not slept in their bed; when the Footmen in the Dining Hall said they had not arrived for their meals; when the Royal Gardeners insisted they had not taken their daily walk in the Gardens; and when the Master of the Horse swore that, no, he had not taken out the Carriages nor driven their Majesties anywhere, nor had he saddled the Royal Horses – then Treece called the Searchers once again. And he asked them to scour the Kingdom for their King and Queen.

But the Searchers could find no one in the entire realm who had seen them. Surely, protested their subjects, their Majesties must be in the capital, ruling Ure as always. Surely they were somewhere in the palace, attending to the affairs of state.

But they were not.

That night Treece tossed and turned in his silken bed. Where could his parents have gone, saying nothing and disappearing utterly? He knew they had been looking for the Wizard. Had they, perhaps, walked off together to see if they could succeed where the Searchers had failed? But how could they have gone on foot, with his mother lame? And without anyone seeing them? It was impossible.

Later that night, none of his problems solved, Treece fell into a troubled sleep. He dreamed, poor Treece, that his mother was calling him. Not just saying 'Treece,' lovingly, the way she had so many times in his life, but sounding so desperate, so filled with fear, that his heart turned over and he awoke.

Moonlight silvered his room. He was wide awake. Yet even awake he could still hear her voice calling and desperate. He longed to help her. 'Mother,' he called back, 'Mother, where are you?'

Then, thinking that his parents had perhaps returned, he ran to the Royal Bedchamber and threw open the door, half expecting to see them in their bed where they should have been. But he was greeted by an eerie emptiness, made all the more empty by the silver moon shining in through one of the tall windows and casting a path of light across the room.

He could still hear his mother's voice, from somewhere, calling, 'Treece. Treece.'

'Tell me where you are and I will come to you,' Treece cried.

And then it was as if the path of moonlight had gathered him up, for there he was on a pearly bar, rising through the night sky in a rush of air.

At first he thought he must be dreaming, for it had happened so suddenly, and nothing in his whole life had prepared him for such an experience. He felt as if he were floating, no longer a prisoner of gravity, and then he realized that he was not floating at all but sitting on something quite firm.

'I am your mother's Fairy Godmother,' a voice said. 'Can I help you?' Beside him stood a being more beautiful than anything he could have imagined.

'Oh, yes!' said Treece. 'At least, I hope you can. My mother is calling me and I don't know where she is or how to find her.'

'I cannot tell you where she is, but I can show you where she went.' The Fairy Godmother led him to the base of a giant tree. 'Look up!' she said.

Unbelieving, he saw a tree, taller than any earthly tree. It seemed to be made of stars and it disappeared into the blackness of the night.

'You will have to climb it,' the Fairy Godmother said. 'That is what your mother did.'

Treece once again wondered if he was dreaming. How could his mother have climbed any tree, let alone this one, when it was difficult for her even to walk. 'Up there?' he asked. 'But how –'

'She climbed,' said the Fairy Godmother. 'And you will have to follow.'

Treece's heart sank. He had no head for heights. As a boy at school he had been ashamed when his friends had run along the railing of the bridge that crossed the river. Every time he had tried to do so his knees had turned to water and his head had spun. Since he had become a young man and, happily, was no longer expected to run along railings, he had put it all out of his mind. But now, his mother needed him and the only way he could reach her was to climb into that vast and terrible space.

Gazing upward, wondering how to begin, he heard his

---

mother's voice again. This time it was high above him, and it was calling, 'Treece! Oh, Treece!'

'Mother, I am here. I am coming.'

Shutting his eyes so that he was unable to see what so terrified him, he jumped for the lowest branch of that blazing tree, and swung himself onto it. He knew that if he looked up into its branches, he would be dazzled by its maze of bewildering lights. And that if he looked down ... but he did not dare look down. So he concentrated intently on climbing and rose from branch to glittering branch.

After what seemed a very long time, he heard his mother's voice again. It was closer now, but weak. And he realized that she was not calling his name as he had thought. She was saying, 'No. No. No. Oh, please. Please!'

'Mother!' he called, 'it's Treece! I am coming.' But as he spoke the lights of the tree went out one by one and in the inky blackness he felt the dizzying emptiness below him and he had to force himself to keep going – gripping the branches firmly and feeling for good footholds as he went. Fingers now clutched at his clothes, pulled at his hair, held him back. From his insecure position in the tree he tried to protect himself. But the fingers he couldn't see tweaked and pinched and were stronger than he was.

'Please!' His mother's voice was hardly more than a whisper.

Treece had no weapon to help him and he was not sure it would have done much good, anyway. He struggled on in the direction of his mother's voice, feeling as if he were trying to swim upstream in a river of air that was full of shoals and snags; and black, blacker than anywhere he had ever been in his life.

After what seemed a long time the Queen's voice sounded again. And this time it was closer still.

'I am coming,' he managed to call. But as he opened his mouth, soft strong fingers filled it. Until now Treece had been

52

uncertain how to fight this unseen enemy, but suddenly he knew it was not enough to protect himself. He must attack. And as he beat and kicked and bit his enemies with all the force left in him, a terrible scream filled the air.

His first thought was that it was his mother's last cry. But when, almost immediately, dozens of hands were plucking, pinching, and holding him – their fingers poking in his ears and eyes – he realized it had been his attacker's scream for help.

Nothing in his life had prepared Treece for what was happening. He had not fought in a war, for there had been no wars to fight; and in the wrestling sports – the nearest he had come to combat as a boy – he had never had to overcome an invisible opponent, or more than one opponent at a time.

Treece's mind was suddenly clear. He knew he had to free his arms and legs for fighting. From his precarious position on a branch he worked his way into a crotch of the tree, leaned against its broad trunk, and fought the only way he could – by biting, scratching, kicking, punching the merciless fingers he could not see. On and on he fought. On and on, until at last he had no strength left. Blackness engulfed him.

He did not know how long it was before he saw a tiny point of light which grew larger and larger, and in its blaze two figures that looked like his mother and father – but young, as young as he was himself. He blinked. It made no sense. His parents were old. His mother walked with a limp and was a little deaf and his father's beard was grey and his face was deeply lined. Yet here they were before his eyes and his mother was beautiful and her hair was black, and his father was like a young athlete with muscular brown arms and legs. And they were no longer wearing their crowns or robes of office. They were clothed in light.

Then Treece realized a remarkable thing. He understood in a flash that everyone in the world was the same age – no one younger or older than anyone else. He could not understand it, but he knew it to be true. Was there something in the air of the world that made people appear to be old or middle-aged or young? And not only people, he thought, but everything living, animals and even fruits.

He had been so surprised by this curious thought and the sight of his youthful parents that he had not noticed the light in which they were flooded was coming from a third figure who glowed from within as if he were a sun. Treece shaded his eyes to gaze at this astonishing golden being. An overwhelming love filled his heart. He knew he was looking at the Wizard. At the same time Treece felt himself pulled towards the Wizard as if by a powerful magnet, and as he joined the three of them in that great, bright space – more beautiful than anything he could have imagined – he was aware that the Wizard and his parents were parts of a whole. And he saw his parents gaze at the Wizard with a wonder and love such as he had never seen. And the same expression was on their faces when they turned to each other.

Treece felt a pang of disappointment as he realized the three of them belonged together, were part of a whole, while he, for some reason he could not understand, was an outsider. Then the Queen looked at Treece as a mother looks at her baby – unbelieving and protective and loving. And in that instant Treece knew that he belonged here, too, that this was his home, just as it was theirs, but that the time had not yet come for him to join them. There was still something he had to do.

'You are now King of Ure, my son,' his father said, turning his youthful face towards him. 'You must return at once, for the court is already preparing for your coronation.' He laughed such a merry laugh that Treece found himself laughing too, even though he barely knew if he was happy or sad.

The King and Queen embraced their son, and Treece understood that before they could meet again he must return to Ure by himself and rule wisely and well as his parents had before him.

Then the Wizard, looking into Treece's eyes, spoke directly to him for the first time. And he repeated the same words he had used to Treece's parents many years ago.

'We shall meet again,' he said.

(1996)

Nãrada's Lesson

Nãrada was a serious maṇ. A good man. Perhaps a godly man. He attended to his prayers, his work, and his family responsibilities. He even found time for his community. All things considered, he was a happy man. But there was a mystery in his life: one he could neither solve nor forget.

His teachers told him the world was illusion – Māyā. His senses told him they were wrong.

Surely the earth beneath his feet was real, and the sky above his head? Was the sun, when it shone, not hot enough to burn him? Did the rain, when it fell, not soak him to the skin? The fragrance of the jasmine blossoms, the taste of his wife's curries … how could they be illusions? To say nothing of the feel of his children's arms around his neck, and his wife's kisses. They were not imagination. Of that he was certain. And yet?

He brooded over this enigma a great deal and finally he raised the subject with his good friend, Kapoor. 'How is it possible,' he asked, 'that everything I touch, taste, smell, hear and see is an illusion? That is what my teacher tells me. It is not that I don't believe my teacher. It is just that I can't believe him.' He kicked a stone and winced at the pain in his toe. Was the pain in his toe not real?

'I see it this way,' his friend replied. 'We have a movie inside us – our movie – in glorious Technicolor with stereo sound. Our eyes are the projector. Everything we see and hear is this movie – everything we think and feel. And because we never leave the cinema, cannot leave the cinema, we believe what we see, and we call it reality. It is, in fact, illusion.'

Nãrada was quiet for a long time. 'If what you say is true,' he said at last, 'then you are part of my illusion. Right?'

'Right!' His friend laughed.

'So what happens to you when you leave my presence? Surely I am not the cause of your existence.'

'Of course not – don't you see? I have a moving picture, too,' Kapoor said.

'And they fit neatly together? Nārada asked. 'Tell me how.' And then, bewildered, 'And what about your wife's movie? And your father's and your mother's and ... and ... and ...' He gave up as the complexity of it overwhelmed him.

'Try not to question everything this way,' his friend said. 'Just accept what our teacher says. Even your questioning is part of Māyā. Our illusions are a spell upon us. Your questions are part of that spell.'

Nārada knew Kapoor was right – for Kapoor. But Nārada was not Kapoor. He had to question things. His very nature seemed to insist upon it.

'Perhaps if I pray more, fast more, practise my devotions more rigorously,' he thought, 'I can learn to question less. And if I question less, perhaps I shall understand.' So Nārada applied himself with greater dedication.

Time passed. Nārada's children grew up. His wife died. With fewer and fewer worldly pressures upon him he became a model devotee, and spent the better part of his days in meditation and prayer. There were even those who considered him a holy man.

But Nārada himself knew that he was not holy, and he was as full of doubts and questions as he had always been.

One day, deep in his usual prayer, he was aware of a sudden light and when he opened his eyes, the god, Vishnu, stood before him. Blazing, like the sun itself.

Was this Māyā? Nārada wondered. Was the god, himself,

part of his dream? But before he had time to wonder further, the god spoke.

'I have come to grant you a wish.'

Nārada had only one wish. One prayer. 'Oh, great Vishnu, show me the magic power of your Māyā.'

'Follow me,' Vishnu replied, and with an inscrutable smile on his beautiful, cruel mouth, he led Nārada from his leafy shelter to a blinding desert that flashed like the blades of swords.

It was hotter than anywhere in Nārada's experience. Even the god himself seemed parched and exhausted. Shielding their eyes and peering into the light, they saw some vague disturbance in the air that might be a distant village.

'Fetch me water,' Vishnu begged.

'Certainly, Lord,' Nārada answered and he set off towards what, as he moved nearer, looked like a cluster of straw huts. But he was uncertain whether it was village or mirage. He was even uncertain whether he was asleep or awake.

Finally, dehydrated and weary, he came to a small hut. To his great relief, the door was solid beneath his knock. A beautiful girl answered and Nārada looked into her eyes. They were the god's eyes.

When she bade him welcome her voice was a silken rope which pulled him into a house so familiar he felt he had lived there forever. He forgot what he had come for. The family members received him with honour and he lived among them as if he belonged, sharing the burdens and joys of their simple life. Before long, to everyone's delight, he married the beautiful girl.

Twelve years passed. During that time the couple had three children, and Nārada assumed his family responsibilities with diligence and love. When his father-in-law died, Nārada became head of the household – managing the estate, tending the cattle and cultivating the fields.

In the twelfth year, the rainy season began with torrential rains. Day after day storm clouds gathered and deluged the plain below. Day after day the despairing villagers tried to patch their leaking roofs and, fearful for their cattle, drove them to the height of land where they herded them into a makeshift corral.

'It must ease up soon,' the villagers told each other. But it did not.

Days turned to weeks and still the rains continued. The people became accustomed to being wet, grew used to the many sounds of water – water dripping, oozing, running, rushing. Small streams overflowed their banks and turned into rivers. The surrounding fields became first a bog, then a vast, shallow lake whose rising waters demolished the makeshift corrals and carried away the pitifully lowing cattle.

With what few possessions they could pack, the desperate villagers struggled to escape. Supporting his wife with one hand, leading the two children with the other, and carrying the baby on his back, Nārada set his face to the driving rain. Darkness fell. It was treacherous underfoot and the current pulled the children along faster than they could walk. Nārada stumbled and the child slipped from his back. In an attempt to save her he let go of the other two and all three were swept away. Before he had regained his own footing his wife's hand was wrenched from his and she too disappeared into the night. If she cried out, he did not hear her above the roaring of the wind and the waters.

Exhausted, and with nothing left to lose, Nārada had neither the heart nor the strength to struggle. Knocked off balance and half drowned, his near-lifeless body – now mere flotsam – was borne along by the rushing current and thrown at the foot of a cliff. When Nārada regained consciousness he could see nothing but a sheet of filthy water in which the straw huts from his village bobbed and swirled, inconsequential as wasps' nests.

Nārada wept.

'Child!' The familiar voice nearly stopped his heart. 'Where is the water you went to fetch for me? I have waited over half an hour.'

Nārada opened his eyes. The glittering, sun drenched desert stretched all around him. Vishnu, the god, was at his shoulder.

'Child,' the god spoke again, the same enigmatic smile on his beautiful, cruel lips, '*now* do you understand the secret of my Māyā?'

(1995)

The Blind Men and the Elephant

A Play for puppets in Two Scenes. **Cast:** 1st Blind Man; 2nd Blind Man; 3rd Blind Man; 4th Blind Man; 5th Blind Man 6th Blind Man; Elephant.

Scene I

(Curtain up on two groups of blind beggars – three on stage left, two on stage right – sitting in front of or leaning against a sunny wall.)

1ST BLIND MAN: How was begging today, brothers?

2ND BLIND MAN: Bad, brother, bad. Two miserable coppers. Barely enough to buy bread.

3RD BLIND MAN: Shake, brother. Only two for me too. But that's two better than yesterday. And who knows? – if Allah wills – tomorrow it may be four.

4TH BLIND MAN: (Entering from stage right. He is excited and waving his white cane.) Abdul, Ali, Rustam – are you there? I bring you good news. The circus has come to town!

2ND BLIND MAN: What's that to us?

A short play based on a fable by the Persian poet Jalaludin Rumi (d.1273).

4TH BLIND MAN: (Enthusiastically) Why, we can go to see it.

2ND BLIND MAN: (Sarcastically) See it!

4TH BLIND MAN: Well, smell it then, hear it. Touch it, even. There are conjurors, fire-eaters, snake-charmers. (Voice rising.) And there's an elephant!

2ND BLIND MAN: An elephant? What on earth's an elephant?

4TH BLIND MAN: You don't know what an elephant is?

1ST BLIND MAN: No. Tell us, brother. Just what is an elephant?

4TH BLIND MAN: Why an elephant is ...

(They all look expectant, encouraging him with *Yeses* and *Is what?*s.)

An elephant is ... an elephant is ... (Triumphantly) ... just what it says. An elephant is an elephant.

2ND BLIND MAN: (Sarcastically) So, an elephant is an elephant. And what, may I ask, is that? Do you eat it? Drink it? Smoke it? Is it animal? Vegetable? Mineral?

5TH BLIND MAN: (Dreamily) I sometimes think an elephant is like a butterfly – beautiful. Or like a sunset. Or like a butterfly against a sunset – the most beautiful thing in the world. I would love to see an elephant!

3RD BLIND MAN: Then why don't we go?

2ND BLIND MAN: Money, brother, money! Just where will we

find the money to get in?

4TH BLIND MAN: (Thoughtful) Let me think ... (Suddenly getting an idea) We'll go tonight when everyone's in bed!

6TH BLIND MAN: Do you think it's safe?

1ST BLIND MAN: I'd rather have a good night's sleep myself. (He laughs) Blind men going to see an elephant. What's the point?

4TH BLIND MAN: (Excited) We can feel it, brother. Feel it! The way we've learned about everything else.

5TH BLIND MAN: (Still dreamily) I'd really like to know if it's like a butterfly.

3RD BLIND MAN: Or a wonderful game or ...

1ST BLIND MAN: For myself, I think a good night's sleep ...

6TH BLIND MAN: Are you sure it isn't dangerous? What if it's a magician who can turn us into snakes or ... or ... (Horrified) ... stones!

4TH BLIND MAN: (Taking command) That's settled then. We shall meet in the elephant's enclosure. At midnight.

(Quick curtain.)

Scene II

(Curtain up on a dark stage. The audience is gradually able to make out an elephant, centre stage, huge; a ladder, stage right; and the 3rd, 5th and 6th Blind Men stage left, near the elephant's head. There is total silence, stillness. Then we see the 4th Blind Man coming over what must be the top of a tent and descending the ladder.)

4TH BLIND MAN: (In a loud whisper as he reaches ground level) Is everybody here?

(They answer, Here, Here, Here.)

Ali and Abdul are always late. Try to be quiet. We don't want to wake anyone.

6TH BLIND MAN: (Nervously) Are you sure we're in the right place?

4TH BLIND MAN: Of course I am. Listen. You can hear it breathing.

(In the silence we hear loud breathing.)

3RD BLIND MAN: (Excitedly) Then ... it's *alive*.

6TH BLIND MAN: I'm leaving. I remember now. Elephants are only about the size of mice but they breathe very heavily. And they're deadly to man. The *least* bite and you're *paralysed*.

(During this speech the 4th Blind Man collides with the front leg of the elephant. He lets out a cry.)

4TH BLIND MAN: (Marvelling) Oh, I touched it. I touched it!

ALL: What's it like. Tell us. Tell us.

(There is silence as the 4th Blind Man feels the leg.)

———

4TH BLIND MAN: (Astonished) Why, it's not alive. There's nothing to fear. An elephant is a great pillar. A column. A tower. Higher than I can reach.

5TH BLIND MAN: Here, give me the ladder. (He props it against the leg.) Let me feel. (He climbs ladder and grabs elephant's ear.) Brothers, brothers, this is no pillar. No column. No tower. It's an enormous fan. Large enough to fan the Sultan himself.

4TH BLIND MAN: (Patient but firm) It's a pillar, I tell you. I touched it. I ought to know.

5TH BLIND MAN: (Still dreamily) Brothers, it's a fan. A beautiful fan. Like the wing of a giant butterfly. I give you my word.

4TH BLIND MAN: (Suddenly exasperated) Is your word better than mine? I touched it I tell you, with these very hands.

(During this argument the 6th Blind Man reaches up and feels the tusk.)

6TH BLIND MAN: (Ominously) Brothers, you are both wrong. I too have touched the elephant. It is a sword: curved, sharp and terrible.

4TH BLIND MAN: I'll sword you. The very idea! It's a pillar, I say.

(Meanwhile the 3rd Blind Man enters. As he feels around he encounters the elephant's tail.)

3RD BLIND MAN: (Delightedly) Brothers, brothers, you are all wrong. A pillar, a fan, a sword! (He laughs) Why, I have an elephant in my hand at this very moment and it is nothing more than a little hanging rope such as children swing on. (He grabs tail and swings.) Whee! Whee! Whee!

(4th and 6th Blind Men continue arguing.)

5TH BLIND MAN: (Dreamily) A fan – like the wing of a giant butterfly. I dreamed it would be so. I knew it all along . . .

(3rd Blind Man continues to swing and cry, Whee!)

1ST BLIND MAN: (Appearing on the elephant's back) You, down there – you're nothing but simpletons – stupid as well as blind. An elephant is a table, a floor, a bed. (He lies down) A perfect place for a snooze.

(During the foregoing the 2nd Blind Man has been feeling about. He encounters the elephant's trunk.)

2ND BLIND MAN: (Very alarmed) Look out, everyone! Stand back! Take care! An elephant is a serpent. A great thick snake, muscled and strong.

5TH BLIND MAN: (To himself) A beautiful fan! I felt it myself. I know what I feel. My senses don't lie.

(The 4th and 6th Blind Men are still arguing. They join the 2nd near the trunk and continue.)

4TH BLIND MAN: A pillar, I say. Tall and straight . . .

6TH BLIND MAN: A sword. A scimitar – curved and sharp.

2ND BLIND MAN: It's a snake, I tell you. I felt its body.

IST BLIND MAN: (From overhead) A perfectly lovely bed. A lovely.... (Snore. Snore.)

(As 'Pillar', 'Sword', 'Snake' and 'Fan' argue and as 'Rope' swings back and forth and 'Bed' snores, the elephant gives a mighty trumpeting. The 1st Blind Man is thrown to the floor and the 3rd lets go its tail and joins the others. Then the elephant lifts his trunk and sprays them all with water. There is pandemonium for a minute or so. After a short silence the refrains begin again.)

4TH BLIND MAN: It's a pillar. I touched it.

6TH BLIND MAN: A sword, I say.

2ND BLIND MAN: A venomous snake.

IST BLIND MAN: A bed.

3RD BLIND MAN: A rope.

5TH BLIND MAN: A beautiful fan!

(And so they continue as the curtain falls. They may even be arguing still.)

The End

Now illuminated, the blind men no longer needed to beg. With such specialized knowledge they were qualified to establish a school of elephantology. The whole world would beat a path ... as they say.

But how present to that world the arcane laws of elephantology to which they were privy – a pillar, a bed, a fan, a hose, a rope, a sword? They asked themselves. They asked each other. Chaos resulted.

Co-operation was impossible. They must separate.

To this day, if you want to learn about elephants you can enrol in one of the many schools: the Pillar, the Bed, the Fan, the Hose, the Rope, the Sword – although already the Hose has split into two schools, bitterly opposed to one another: the Hose and the Whip.

(1970s)

Even the Sun, Even the Rain

Robert, looking frail and old after his last illness, collected her nevertheless and they drove up to the lookout.

They had not been there since they were young lovers and today the snow was still on the ground around them though the city itself was through with it. They peered at the maquette of buildings below. Those that had been giants when they were young were now hidden by massive plinths.

He talked of the death of the city and she thought how they were dying together – he and his city. She could give him no comfort by her long view – that another city would rise up, was rising up, to replace this one; that the young who were having to leave because work was no longer available would go elsewhere and that *that* elsewhere – or those – would surge and grow.

They walked over to the great neglected building that had once housed a restaurant. Couples lay about on its steps in the sun, the first warm sun of the year, and he walked carefully between them, she following.

He said, 'Have you ever seen the steps of the Capitol in Washington, on a fine day?' and the contrast was painful to her in a way she was unable to understand.

They walked into the vast, empty, unswept hall. Two dispensing machines against the far wall provided the only colour, were the only objects. He offered her a chocolate bar which she refused, thinking of calories. He put coins in the slot and pulled the plunger.

'A little energy,' he said.

He was pale and there were small hairline veins in his cheek that she had not seen before. His mouth fell open as if it cost him too much to keep it closed. The lower lip was slack but the skin was stretched taut and shiny. It was an old man's mouth.

They sat on the steps in the sun and she talked about the three brains – reptilian, mammalian, the neocortex – and their possible functions. He questioned her on the biological sound-ness of the theory and, laughing, she told him she thought there were three brains, all right. But there was some niggling unease between them. After all, just because they had known each other for forty years and loved each other for forty years it didn't mean they could fall into step immediately when they met. It always took time. Not a lot of time, but time, especially after so long an interval as this one had been.

They walked slowly back to the car past the piles of dirty snow and drove down to the city where he parked recklessly in a no-parking area. 'A calculated risk,' he said, and she knew it was a matter of energy.

Lunch was delicious – *dorée amandine*, green salad, white wine. He grew flushed with the martini – 'the first since my ill-ness' – and easier.

'I was frightened of seeing you,' he said.

A young man passed their table, stared hard at Robert, was about to speak, saw her and stared harder at her. Stared at Robert again, introduced himself and moved on.

'He wondered if we were the right couple,' Robert said.

'How could you *ever* be frightened of seeing me?'

'The mountain is so enormous it's hard to be anywhere but the top.'

'Take it as it comes,' she said. 'Wherever we are will do – even on the slopes.'

His usual high spirits returned. But he ate very slowly, so she talked to give him time to eat.

'Extraordinary to be so slow. But it won't go down faster.'

Quite suddenly they were in step again. They were holding

hands tightly under the table.

'Had you better put your feet up?' she asked. 'You can drop me wherever you like.'

'How about 203?'

She was surprised. Enough for her eyes to go a shade lighter. She had expected him to go home.

He had a ticket, of course. He pocketed it without a glance. 'Well worth it,' he said.

Once in the car they wanted to buy each other books – all the books they had talked about. It was an old pattern. He headed towards a book shop but the streets were thick with traffic.

'Too complicated,' she said. 'Let's buy them later and send them.'

He drove to her hotel – careful in all those roaring cars. Parked, again illegally. Inside her hotel room they took off their clothes and lay beside each other on the bed.

'Even the sun is not like this,' he said.

'Or the rain. Rain is also something.'

'Even the rain....'

The old joy filled them.

'I call it subliming,' she said. 'Funny that all these years I've never told you.'

(1999)

Birthday

After the effort of dressing – and it was an effort these days, quite exhausting, in fact – she needed to pause a little, compose herself, before beginning the day. The chair she sat in, like a burnished throne, shone brightly in the sun and there she rested, burnished too, and the glitter of her rings transformed the morning.

Sometimes she wondered if the chair and the sunlight – perhaps especially the sunlight – contributed to or even hatched, the fragments of knowledge which slipped into her head from the side, glancing through her, leaving a trace like the silvery trail of a snail or which, more directly, arrived head-on – shooting stars, illuminating but transitory.

So far she had been unable to attach meaning to these glimmerings and flashes, palely glowing; she might even say, 'burning sweetly', in the space in her head where her brain had once been but where, now, it was as if her heart were tenant.

What was she to make, for instance, of the knowledge that she was awaiting an event, one which – she now realized – she had been awaiting since birth? Perhaps before. Possibly even before. As to the nature of the event or what prompted its knowledge, she hadn't the least idea.

Was its source, she wondered, some quickening in the air – the same quickening one feels as the old year draws to its close? Or, perhaps she had been programmed – she was amused by her change in vocabulary, for surely, she once would have said 'influenced' – by images from all her forgotten dreams. Were her changing cells simply bypassing the 'operator' entirely and dialling direct to the 'listener' within? Here, she could only speculate.

But she knew time was short. Knew it certainly. Knew the event near and beyond question. And even though it had no form, no detail, and she possessed no clues as to what it was, she couldn't rid her mind of it. It was there that her thoughts centred – electrons circling a nucleus. At times it was as if the electrons were becoming an entity in themselves and gradually replacing what she had always thought to be – for want of a better word – herself. For surely it was not she who, yesterday, threw out the eyedrops that control glaucoma? Even less would she have refused, stubbornly refused, the analgesic which eased the pain of arthritis. Something other than herself must be in control.

Was it simply that she was old and scatty? she asked. For she was old, after all, and strangely changed, on the surfaces at least. For proof she need look no further than her rheumaticky hands, wrinkled and blotched like snakeskin, the fingers swollen and twisted. The knuckles shiny. But as she examined them in the bright sunlight, she knew quite clearly that in no time at all they would be the tiny, soft, rubbery, red fists of a baby. Involuntarily her stomach jerked. It was rather as she had felt when first she knew that she was something other than her body; that although it was flesh that made her visible, she was not that flesh. No wonder her stomach jerked: flesh objects to playing so secondary a role.

And then she remembered the dream. Those little red fists had brought it back. It was bizarre, of course. One's dream scenarist tends to be antic.

Head foremost, she was forcing – and at the same time being forced – down a long book-lined corridor. Books on both sides. How tight it made the passage! Painful. Cramped. Intolerable, actually. And an area between her shoulder blades – not usually one of her more sensitive spots, though she had many these days – was unbearably tender. But as she struggled, constricted, half blind, she was comforted by a series of brilliant images: butterfly; bird; man; angel. Her own joyous laughter had wakened her that morning. She remembered it now with a matching lightness of heart.

Suddenly curious, she tried to touch that spot between her shoulders. The pain in wrists and elbows hindered her movements. But when the fingers of a persistent right hand finally succeeded, she was rewarded by the discovery of two protuberances – ridge-shaped – one on either side of her spine, and agonizingly sensitive to the touch. For, added to the accustomed pain of arthritis, was the suddenly remembered torture of teething and the unique realization of the distress and ecstasy of the unicorn as a foal when, cutting his horn, he perceived that he was not the young horse he had thought himself to be.

A long arm of sunshine reached out and fell upon the glinting aglets of a pair of narrow shoes. Her brother was standing just inside the door – thin, aquiline, smiling. How many years was it since she had seen him? 'Robert!' she cried, 'how good of you to come.'

'It's Victor,' a voice answered. 'Your son and heir. You've forgotten, Mother. I was here yesterday.'

Yesterday? Ah Robert, Victor, time does bear thinking about, doesn't it. Passing without notice when it wishes or travelling at the speed of light. And what time was it, that she should now be lying here in her bed? Indeed, what day? She reached out to the sun's pale, fine dust that lay like a ribbon on her blanket and with the jolt she had come to know as certainty, she realized that this was her last awakening in this bed, this room, this ... 'place'.

Could the wintry sunlight, starting with her fingers, dissolve her flesh, her bones, all matter? For, light as thistledown, she and the material world were suspended, painless, totally detached. The cord that had bound her to all she loved was severed, she thought, forever. What possible links could survive this atomization?

Yet links survived. Her sight – better today than usual –

took in the bare boughs of trees, their colour a nameless dark against the sky. It was as if she had never seen them before, yet their diffuse forms were as familiar to her as the bed she lay in. Her mind was clear too – startlingly clear – for she actually saw the two contradictions arise as one and separate and become two as if they had passed through a prism or fragmenter. 'But it's not only opposites which are born single and become dual,' she thought excitedly. 'More complex still, any image, at a certain point, will splinter and multiply.'

Eager to test this new perception – 'tree', she thought and immediately it was sawn into planks, hammered into coffins, shaped into violins, pressed into paper. She could not hold 'tree' in her mind singly, simply. The one became two, three, four or even more. And this propensity to fragment had been, she now knew, central to her life. Not her life only, of course. It was in the nature of humankind. And she was on the brink of controlling it. All she had to do was allow a stop to occur at exactly the right moment – no more difficult than releasing the shutter of a camera when the light, speed, focus and subject were all correctly aligned. But the art of doing it vanished along with a certain radiance the room had contained and there she was again, an old body on a bed, faced with the imminence of the event and shaky. Shaky.

'Oh, I would go back on the whole thing if I could,' she said, knowing that she couldn't, but not why.

'When was the decision made and by whom?' she demanded. 'Was I a conscious party to it? Was it my wish?'

'I suppose it's like waiting to die,' she thought. 'The same uncertainty about what is to come, the same fear of pain, the same wrench from the known. But,' she queried, 'being born where? In what country? With what planets rising? And what colour?' she asked herself idly. But as to that, she was only mildly curious, for no part of her cared whether or not she continued white.

'The same with size,' she went on, 'although that, I suppose, might embrace differences other than those measurable in feet and inches. But I'd adjust,' she said, confident. 'Alice did, after all. Took her changes with remarkable *sang froid* – a reflection of the age and race to which she belonged, perhaps.'

'But sex,' she thought with a stab, 'is another matter.' Appallingly repellent, the mere idea of being male. Not that she hadn't loved male flesh well enough in her time. 'Too well,' she thought, nostalgically. But the prospect of *being* it ... the stubble, the muscle, the hair on the chest ... the Adam's apple ... No! 'I wouldn't know how to be male,' she exclaimed aloud. 'I'm so at home in this female body.' But as she spoke she realized that she wasn't at home in it any more. Nearly all of it was painful to her – a stricture – especially in that area between the shoulder blades. In fact, since the appearance of those two new ridges, it was impossible for her to lie on her back, and her bed was a rack and a harrow.

'More important,' her thoughts were racing now, reminiscent of the descriptions of the speed of flying saucers – 'vastly more important even than gender – or nationality or colour or size – is kind.' What if she were born in the body of a dog, for instance? Not that there weren't exceptional dogs. But it would be disappointing and repetitive, for on the evolutionary scale she must already have been a dog or its equivalent, must already have managed four hairy legs and a tail, and it would be a matter simply of doing it all over again.

But curious dislocations were occurring within her and without. Reassemblies. She was no longer ... in place. From this great height, she could barely make out towers or steeples, and geometry, which she had studied so eagerly as a girl, was now either pre- or post-Euclidean. Its angles altered. 'Michael, Raphael, Gabriel,' she said. 'All male. And Uriel. Male also.' And despite the fact that her mind surged and flowed and she seemed able to draw upon the whole of creation as if from a meticulously indexed encyclopaedia, she couldn't recall a single female angle.

Such vast accessibilities without. So great a condensation within. A gathering together, a coalescence. Heightened inertia. 'Bend back thy bow, O Archer ...'

'What matter,' she asked, 'if I die female and am born male? Through the alembic of this giant eye, male/female are won.'

And as the fragmenter or prism in her mind reversed direction, all multiplicity without – the trail of the snail, the shooting stars, the baby, the tree, her brother, her son – was, through its unifying beam, drawn into her to become again what it had always been and was still – hole, won; and this same reversal made possible the contraction of all her particles as if in preparation for rising – a spacecraft taking off. And through one supra sense she heard the rush of air, and through that same sense – upstream of the five now left behind in a fractured world – she felt the exquisite movement of its currents stirring the small down on her incredible wings.

(1985)

Victoria

Victoria claims my memory of the event is not memory at all but imagination. And I wonder. Not only whether she is correct, but about the very nature of the two. Is imagination perhaps a further, longer memory? A remembering outside time, beyond space?

(*Do you remember*, I say to my very old aunt, frail as lace in her hospital bed, *do you remember me?* Her eyes are clear and shining as peaty water. *No*, she says. *Do you remember*, I try again, *your garden at Blythe?* Her eyes narrow, she looks far off and – *No*, she says. *Do you remember...?* But she cuts me short. *I don't remember anything, any more.* Then, *Perhaps you remember*, I suggest, playful, pressing, *time before you were born?* And, *That would perhaps be easier*, she says.)

Although the question in dispute concerns our first meeting, Victoria would, I am sure, agree that I didn't imagine her. Is she not real enough to argue? To put me straight? Sufficient proof, surely, to her at least, that she is no figment of my imagination. And if not she, then why the others?

I remember her first as a child, pink-coated, plump, glued – as it were – between the angular navy-blue serge figures of her parents. She was small but not altogether young, staring enquiringly through the thick glasses she wore even then. The occasion, a prize-giving for which she had come in from the country, fresh from the butter-and-cream-coloured flowers of her prize-winning painting. Her father, awkward in his best suit, her mother curiously girlish in her pale straw hat. And she, Victoria, short, self-contained, self-centred even; hair cut straight and square above those bright eyes. Dark as a robin's and like a robin's, expectant. Intent. As intent then as now. She panned the room – an intelligent camera – taking in that great warehouse of a studio, its visible walls covered with paintings of nudes and still-lifes, its far walls lost, dissolved by the faint light of the candles.

We were young. Dream-filled. But we must have looked old to her. We smoked. We drank. Neither she nor her parents did either. We had not expected her quite so young, so chaperoned. From so different a world where work was a physical, manual affair that enlarged the hands, lined and roughened the skin.

The group they formed, the three of them standing there in the smoke-thickened air, set them apart. They might have been a piece of sculpture, a painting. In Victoria, the mother's fair colouring merged with the father's features to make a pale, female, juvenile version of the swarthy man whom she would, I felt sure, come to resemble more strongly as the years passed. I saw them very clearly with my painter's eye: the echoing family likenesses, the vivid pink of Victoria's coat repeated – faded – in the flowers on her mother's hat. The two dark forms flanking – protecting? – their bright bud. I saw them clearly then as I see them clearly still. They are printed sharply on my retina – those three short figures outside fashion and city ways, outside pretension, set down in our youthful bohemia. Real, in a way we weren't.

We presented Victoria with her prize. Pleased, but not unduly so, was the impression they gave – either by her talents or our bounty. One did what one did and took the consequences – good or bad. Such was their attitude. Their presence, alien among us, just happened to be the consequence of Victoria's painting. If they disapproved of us they gave no sign. If they envied us it was not apparent.

And having done what they came to do, they departed,

leaving where they had stood a seemingly unfillable space which for a time we walked around as if they were still there.

Victoria insists – certain her memory is more accurate than mine – that she came to the studio right enough, but *alone*; having journeyed by train through the prairie landscape *alone*. (She is firm in her emphasis.) And that she spent the night at the house of one of the competition judges. Damnably, she even remembers her name.

(*Do you remember your name?* I question my aunt, pinched in her hospital bed and cranked up so that she folds in the middle. *Yes,* she replies, looking at me as if I were trying to trick her. *It's Woodhouse. The house I live in.* And, *Do you remember mine?* Eagerly I pursue the reviving memory, close in. She looks at me as if she had never seen me before. Mute. *It's Gail,* I say. *Gail,* she repeats. *Is that the house you live in?* Perhaps it is.)

Victoria laughs at me when I speak of her parents, maintaining that I have always had more imagination than she. She speaks of me with a curious familiarity as if she knows me and my ways. She tells me of our correspondence during the period she spent in the sanatorium. I recall nothing of all this. She says she has my letters to prove it. Then prove it, I say. How otherwise can I know that in what she is pleased to call her memory, my letters are not just as much imagined by her as her parents – so she still contends – are imagined by me?

With age she is longer, leaner, sparer altogether than the child's frame would have led one to expect. The likeness to her father is now striking. Hair cropped and brushed back reveals his high brow, once hidden by her little-girl bangs. The intent glance, in no way diminished, is nevertheless modified by some passivity, some willingness to be observer – a role which, thirty years ago, had already stamped the features on her father's face. If time has so emphasized this resemblance, as indeed it has, was I not – on that prize-winning night – rather more prophetic than imaginative? And if the very model itself was the product of my imagination, how has she now grown so perfectly to match it?

(My aunt has taken her spoon and delicately, incomprehensibly, is working among the petals of the hydrangea on her table. *What are you doing?* I ask, watching her eyes, her fingers, the silver flashing silver-blue in the purple-blue of the flower. She doesn't look at me. *I'm not hurting it,* she replies, defensive. *I am only trying to remove the issue.* She pronounces the word in the old-fashioned way, the double 's' a whistled hiss, the 'u' French. *Is it difficult?* I inquire. *No, it's quite easy but I can't do it. You just very gently force it apart and remove the issue. It doesn't hurt it at all,* she says. *And what do you want it for?* I ask, interested. *To paint the shadow of that star that is shining there.*)

Victoria's paintings – whatever the subject – remain for me like the flowers of her childhood. Innocent, literal, freshly seen. Uncompromisingly honest, the critics say. Honest as far as she goes, I am tempted to amend. For what, after all, is this immediate reality we stub against but the first obvious gate opening onto a further reality? A reality Victoria would undoubtedly call imagination.

We have painted together from time to time over the years on those rare occasions when we are both in the same city – she working from the model before her, the possibility of altering it never entering her mind; I working from nothing visible, as a spider making its web. Both of us silent, engrossed. *You are more imaginative than I,* she says, and *You've caught it exactly,* I reply.

So here we are after half a century of intermittent meetings, she so sure of the reality before her nose; I like Chuang-Tze, not knowing dream from reality, imagination from dream.

Am I now, at this very moment, no more than the product of Victoria's unremembered dream? Or did I, all those years ago, imagine not only the father she resembles and the mother whose colouring she shares, but the little Victoria – Victoria herself?

(For my aunt, the cosmos has entered her sickroom. The angels crowding her move soft as swans. Their wings are elegantly folded knife-pleat linen, their shining faces, the faces of her friends. They are gentle with her, fingering her worn flesh. *They won't hurt,* I assure her. *They're only removing the issue.* And although I have to put my ear to her lips because there is so little breath left, the words are quite distinct and full of wonder. *Have I an issue to remove?* she says.)

(1976)

As One Remembers a Dream

I t was years since Sadie had put the question directly to her mother. But as if it were yesterday she remembered waking that Saturday morning, stringing the words together into a sentence and carrying them around with her all day. Remembered following her mother from room to room as she dusted and cleaned, waiting, hoping for the moment to come when it would be easy.

'Run outside and play, Sade,' her mother had said more than once. 'Go along now, there's a love.'

And outside it was beautiful. She had *wanted* to go out. Had wanted to push a hole right through the wall and break free from the house, her mother, her whole life. But the chain of words had held her on a long tether, wandering from room to room, silent. Then having left it to the last possible moment when she could safely be alone with her mother, when, at any minute, she might hear her father's footsteps on the porch, she had walked into the kitchen and the great urgency of the question was like a wound.

Her mother was peeling potatoes at the sink and the late afternoon sun shone in the window and made the knife blade glint and reflect in a dancing pattern on the wall. Sadie had crept into the room like a culprit and stood, unspeaking.

'What are you doing, Sade?' Her mother spoke without turning and Sadie had felt embarrassed, guilty almost, as if she were about to ask where babies came from or ...

'Have you lost your tongue, child?'

She must ask it now. If she waited another minute it would be too late.

'Mum!' The whole kitchen revolved, making her dizzy.

'What's the matter with my foot, Mum? My foot, Mum. What's the matter with it? Mum? Mum!'

It wasn't as she had planned to say it. The words had tumbled out, making a great racket in the unsteady room and then leaving it silent except for the little plop as peeled potatoes were dropped in the pot of water. Her mother's hands had continued moving as she said, 'Now don't you mind about that, Sade. Light the gas for me, there's a good girl, or tea won't be ready for your dad.'

'But I'm old enough to know. I want to know. It's not fair.' Her voice had wailed on the last word and her mother had popped the last potato in the pot, run her hands down her apron with a small exhalation of accomplishment and said, 'There's nothing the matter that the boot won't fix, my beauty.'

That was years ago. And it was today. Both. She had outgrown three pairs of boots since then and was well into her fourth – black, hideously corrective things that laced half way up her calf.

Time before the boots was non-existent. She couldn't force her memory back at all, except, of course, for that one thing, isolated, different in quality from anything else that had ever happened, and that she remembered occasionally as one remembers a dream. It was a detailed, untouchable thing, floating, forming, fading – crystallizing as sharply and vividly as cut glass – and as suddenly disappearing before it finished – disappearing easily and finally as clouds fade in a blue sky. When it came, it came from nowhere and always, no matter how hard she tried to hold on, it left again, incomplete. The important thing about it was that then – or there – there were no boots. Then or there she had left a pair of sandals under a green tree in order to follow Justy. The grass had pricked the soles of her feet and Justy had yelled impatiently, 'Come onnn!' Boots had no place in that picture. If only she could turn around where she stood and retrace her own steps to the original pair – to the moment before them, rather – she felt she could cancel them out. They wouldn't be true. Or if she could force someone to mention her foot – by some violence on her part – a further mutilation of it perhaps – then, the mere objective acknowledgement would settle the thing finally, one way or the other.

She wore the boots over navy blue socks, the high kind that come up to the knee and fold over showing a design. Her mother bought them for her, all the same, ribbed and dark with a lot of grey dots for a pattern. At sixteen she hated them more than the boots. At sixteen all the kids at school were wearing silk stockings. She had glanced at her legs beneath the desk – calves the colour of ink – and with her history book propped up in front of her and gazing steadily at the Fathers of Confederation, she had rolled the socks down as one would over ski boots. She knew her legs would be a sickly white but she didn't care. And if her mother said anything she had prepared her answer. But her mother said nothing at all.

Sometimes she tried to catch her mother off guard, mentioned cases of polio and watched her mother's face as she spoke; told stories she had heard at school of monsters being born because their mothers had been frightened or had fallen or suffered from shock. She learned to say these things casually, as if it were weather she spoke of, all the time gazing with apparently indifferent eyes, waiting for the start, the blush, the nervous betraying movement. But her mother replied, 'Poor little mites,' or, 'Sade, where in the world do you hear such stories? Upon my word, I've never heard of such things in my life.' And then the memory would return, or the dream, of her own legs running, grass green and soft beneath a tree where apples large and red as balloons hung in clusters or dropped with a thud into their hands, and how the sky became, that day, not a fixed thing, miles away, but something close and blue, almost within reach. And how she had left her sandals under the tree, eager to catch up with Justy.

But now she was folding towels in a laundry, working for a living. Grown up. Now she would tolerate the socks no longer. Now with her own money she could buy stockings, silk ones like the other girls wore. And now people were nothing but legs and feet. The street cars and street were full of them, all shapes and colours and sizes. In her mind she chose the stockings she would have – beautiful, filmy, honey-coloured – scorning legs less perfectly clad. She was critical, pitying, amused by turns at the wrinkles, the runs, the textures and tones of the stockings that passed. She cut stocking ads from magazines and stuck them in her mirror, half believing that if she looked at them long enough, often enough, a miracle might happen. And she treated her socks with a certain deference now that she was going to discard them. Folded them carefully at night as if to make up for the day when she would ruthlessly ignore them.

The day she received her first pay envelope she went straight for the stockings after work. People crowded the counter, pushed in ahead of her, were irritable, casual, bored. She leaned on the counter dreaming, growing up. The amputated legs of a dummy waved above her head. She viewed them as a connoisseur; they were neither grotesque nor humorous.

The salesgirl's voice sounded brusquely beside her: 'Yes? Yes?'

She smiled. Her excitement lay upon her like oil on water. 'Some silk stockings, please.'

'We have no silk. Haven't had since the war started.'

For a moment she was bewildered. Then the salesgirl pushed a box across the counter saying nothing, arranging her curls instead, unrolling them and twisting them up again over her fingers and pushing them into place like so many small sausages in a double row. She looked from the salesgirl to the stockings, slipped a pair from the box. They were copper coloured and shiny. They wouldn't do at all.

'You've nothing else?'

The salesgirl shook a disinterested head.

'But the colour ...'

'That's the popular shade right now. Take them to the light.'

She limped off with them in her hands, feeling their slippery texture. By the street door they looked a little better but they still weren't right. Not what she wanted.

Back at the counter she asked, 'How much?'

'A dollar twenty-five.'

It was a lot of money. She hesitated. The salesgirl was brushing off her dress, licking her fingers and rubbing.

'Will you be getting others? Others – different?'

'We may. You never know. This may be the last shipment for weeks.'

If she waited she might never get a pair. If ... 'All right,' she said and counted the money carefully.

There was no chance to try them on before tea. No chance at all, in fact, until she was going to bed. But a wonderful thing had happened after she bought them: the simple fact of ownership transformed them, made them perfect. All evening she had thought of them in a new way. *My* stockings, she had thought. Mine. The pronoun changed them into the stockings she had imagined.

In her room she waited until she heard her mother's bed springs creak before she took them from the paper bag. Dad was still up but he never barged in, anyway. She laid them over the back of the wooden chair. They hung down silken, flat, while she undressed. She unlaced the hideous boots with her fingers trembling, pulled off the horrible socks and flung them in a corner and then, with the clumsy, unsure reverence of the novice, slipped the long, weightless stockings onto her legs. She lay back on her bed and held her good leg up, gripping the top of the stocking to keep it taut, seeing a future of slim, silk, adult legs. She thought of her mother in the next room, a familiar stranger, her thin body stretched out on her half of the double bed, her rectangular flat hand laid across her eyes. The years of her mother's secrecy and silence had built towards this time when understanding was atrophied, when nothing could be shared. Her mother would ignore the stockings too, Sadie had no doubt. And she felt suddenly bitter imagining them ignored, realizing how not only her failures but her victories would go unacknowledged; how forever and ever her mother would make the land dead level by the simple act of not seeing, pretending not to see, saying nothing.

Quietly Sadie took the mirror from the wall and propped it against her dresser, walked away from it, towards it, turned it on its side for a broader reflection as she walked past it. Next she tried on her boots, laced them carefully, rubbed them up a bit with a piece of Kleenex and walked towards the mirror again. They were solid and ugly as iron. Hideous and heavy over the stockings as they had never been over the socks. They were so hideous that she couldn't look at them. She turned her back in quick revulsion, held her hand across her eyes in a gesture identical with her mother's. In a sudden violent need for action she reached for the scissors and cut the laces all the way down, tore the boots from her feet and threw them across the room, the noise of misery sounding so loudly in her ears that she didn't hear the two thumps they made as they fell. Exhausted, she slumped on the bed. The breath in her lungs was an amorphous solid, hard, difficult to move.

Nothing was said about the laces next morning, not even when Sadie said, 'I cut them. Cut them.'

Busy buttering toast her mother replied, 'You'll find another pair in the left-hand drawer of my sewing cabinet. Go and get them like a good girl.'

Obediently she had gone for the laces, stooped and threaded their licorice lengths into the boots. In and out through the holes, criss-crossing and tightening, ascending higher and higher up her legs and her fingers moved with them as if climbing laboriously to the tops of two black and sinister ladders. It was then that her mind took a large leap, the extent of which astonished her. It was audacious beyond words, yet so simple, natural. Once having made it she wondered only that it had not occurred to her before.

She would buy shoes. Other people bought them. Wonderful, high-heeled shoes without toes. Shoes with bows, perhaps, platform soles. She saw the thousands of towels she would have to fold before it was possible. Great mounds and mountains of towels and the movements her arms would make folding them. But she saw it all speeded up, so that the towels flew about in the air like a snow storm and the days shrank to half their length as she worked with the vision of the shoes before her.

There was another thing too that occupied her mind at this time. It was the dream. Always before, the dream had been something of her own, private and personal, but now, thinking about it, really thinking about it, not just letting it flow past her, Justy established himself as part owner. He was a real person with a name. Justy Williams. A dream figure no longer. If she could just find Justy Williams, find him and talk to him. Yet he had existed only once so far as she knew; once long ago beneath a tree, eating apples when the sky came low down just over the trees, curving blue. So low you could almost touch it.

'Has anyone ever touched the sky?' she asked.

Justy was scornful. 'No one couldn't ever touch the sky.'

'I bet they could too.' And staring at it, it went all funny. It came down low and then it went up high again. She held up her arm as she said, 'With a ladder I bet I could. I bet I could get a whole handful on a ladder.'

'Oh, maybe with a ladder,' Justy had allowed.

The spire rose up then, right into the sky. She could see where it touched. She sat up, pointing. 'If I was up there I could touch it.'

———

Justy looked. His eyes grew big. 'Geee! I bet I could touch the sky if I was up there,' he said as if it was his idea. 'Come on.'

They ran over to the church. A tree growing beside it spread one branch close to the roof. Justy threw his apple core at the wall of the church, hitched his pants up firmly and began to climb. She watched him clamber up the trunk, go out on his stomach along the branch and swing onto the roof.

'S'easy. Come on.'

She couldn't get a start on the trunk with her sandals. They were slippery so she took them off and put them in the grass under the tree. The rough bark tickled the soles of her feet as she climbed. When she tried to wriggle along the branch as Justy had, her dress caught, so she stopped and tucked it into her pants. She had swung herself onto the roof beside him saying, 'Gee, that was easy.' Looking down the world had flowered green all around her for miles and miles. It must have been then that she had decided God couldn't see so much after all. It had never struck her before how she had come to that conclusion. But it must have been then, on the church roof. From so high up He couldn't see anything at all but trees and houses and maybe processions.

The more she thought about the dream the more it changed. It was undreamlike now. Her background, her past, something solid and real which grew into her present, linked up with it and made it what it was.

That night at tea she put a straight question to her parents: 'Where's Justy Williams now?'

She wondered if she detected a slight stiffening in her father. She had tried to watch them both at the same time. Her father's eyes had certainly turned to her mother's but he might well have been appealing to his wife to jog his memory, as he invariably did.

'Justy Williams?' her mother murmured questioningly. 'Justy Williams? I don't know any Justy Williams.'

'The kid I used to play with when I was little.' Sadie was merciless. 'The kid who climbed onto the church roof with me. We had a fight up there because we both wanted to be God and two people couldn't be God. So we fought about it.' She laughed. It had suddenly become funny. And her mother laughed too.

'You must have dreamed it all, Sade. I don't know what you're talking about.'

Her father was interested. 'Who won the fight?' he asked.

'Oh, Justy, I guess. I said there could be two Gods, there could even be three – God the Father, God the Son and God the Holy Ghost. So we stopped fighting for a while to think it over and then Justy said, "Well, *you* can't be God the Father or God the Son because you're a girl. You'll have to be God the Holy Ghost." I had to give in to that, so I guess he won. Then he started yelling, "I'm God the Father. I'm God the Son." And I kept yelling, "I'm God the Holy Ghost."'

Her father leaned back in his chair and laughed so that his stomach shook. 'That's rare,' he said. 'God the Son,' he spluttered. 'God the Holy Ghost!' He put his hands over his face and heaved. 'Ho, ho, ho,' he laughed. 'That's rare all right!' And then he pulled his face together and only smiled and his eyes darted about a bit, not knowing where to settle. But the wild humour of it struck him again and his body began to jiggle and rock and the laughter poured out of him as if it had been pent up too long.

Sadie didn't think it so funny now. He had sucked the humour out of it with all that laughter. She looked at her mother who was shaking her head quietly, patiently.

'What a man your father is for a joke,' she said. 'He'd even laugh at the Lord God Himself. Here,' she reached out and plucked her husband's sleeve. 'Leave off,' she said.

'What I want to know,' said Sadie, relentless, 'where's Justy Williams now?'

Her parents' eyes met again.

'I never heard tell of that name before,' said her father. He fidgeted a moment with his spoon. Then, 'God the Son!' he spluttered and was off again, laughter owning him, distorting him. And the subject was lost once more.

Sadie realized that the route to Justy was blocked, cemented up. Her entire past lay beyond her parents, but through them there was no road. Or even, conceivably, and far worse, a series of blind roads. Their strategy was so subtle and their signposts so numerous that at any moment she could be misled without suspecting it. She could no longer trust them at all. Neither their evasions nor their clues. Her immediate reaction was to leave the maze they had built around her. Walk out. But a maze is not a thing you can leave at once. And she was tied by her foot. It had replaced the umbilical cord. If she could only alter the foot, alter the boots … It would be months before she could save enough money for shoes but once she had it she would walk out, out and away to that memory of freedom, that recollection or fantasy – she couldn't be sure which – that stopped so abruptly on the church roof. Vivid to that point and then blank.

When finally she did have the money for the shoes she couldn't bring herself to buy them. The importance of the purchase was so tremendous that she put it off. It was the giant step from lame dependence into the world she had dreamed of, a world she already knew by its flavour through and through. The fact that she now had the money seemed to place the shoes further out of reach than when they were urgent, vital and impossible. The very fact that there was nothing to stop her was the very fact that stopped her. She waited, lost, seeking some sign, some indication that the correct moment had come, until passing a shop one day she walked in as naturally as if she had been buying shoes all her life.

Once inside she felt split – child and grown-up simultaneously. The memory of Justy which accompanied her reduced her to the size she had been on the day when they had made their way across the roof to the spire. At its base there was a ledge which she could just reach with her fingers if she jumped. It was firm beneath her grip but she couldn't pull herself up. 'Push me!' she called to Justy.

The sales clerk came forward. He was young with pimples and as he bent down to unlace her boots he seemed familiar to her, reminding her of someone. She must be imagining, but he reminded her of Justy.

'I want some shoes,' she said and saw herself dangling.

'Any particular style?'

Justy's hands shoved from beneath. It was funny how it seemed to be happening together – climbing the steeple and buying the shoes. It was mixed, like a dream again.

Above the ledge the base sloped and above the sloping part the slender little spire rose high into the sky. She crawled gingerly up the incline, balancing carefully. Justy – the clerk, she meant – was measuring her feet on a kind of ruler. He made a wry face and she heard Justy's voice yell, 'Watch out!' she climbed higher and higher and grabbed the spire. The clerk went into the back of the store and while she waited she saw herself clearly wrapping her legs as far round the spire as they'd go and starting to shinny up it. It was hard work and the sun beat down on her head like a hammer.

The clerk emerged again from the back of the store. He grinned like Justy and held a pair of spectators on the palm of one hand. She felt a great surge of excitement rise in her and almost choke her. She held out her hands for them and as she did so, realized that she was well above the level of the base. If she let go with one hand and reached up she could touch the sky easily. Carefully, shifting her weight, she tightened the pressure of her right arm, preparatory to releasing the left.

The clerk said, 'Shall we try them on?' With the help of a shoehorn he slipped one onto the good foot. It was perfect.

The sky was right there, she knew. She held her free hand above her head, calling, 'Justy! Look! I'm touching it. I'm touching the sky.' She could tell by the feel. It was soft, swirling, blue.

The clerk slipped the toe of the shoe onto the bad foot and tried to force it on. He struggled and she wriggled her foot to help. But as she wriggled she felt herself slipping, losing her grasp on the steeple, and she heard Justy yell and the clerk say, 'I'm sorry. I was afraid of that. There won't be no shoes that will fit. You see ...'

She nodded. There was nothing she could say. But she had time as she fell to watch him as he laced up her boots and tied the bows with a final quick jerk. 'I'm sorry,' he said again. 'I'm very sorry.'

All emptiness embraced her. 'Thank you Justy,' she said, and she felt the swirling blue currents of the air as it rushed by.

(1946)

The Woman

I n the small villages in the darkness all the square, flat-fronted hotels were shut. Inquiries brought forth the reply that they closed on Sundays. And the traveller? Doomed to a chromium-fitted night in a city; doomed to enter lonely into lobbies where charwomen with mops and brushes worked among palms and ashtrays filled with sand.

No. John renounced the idea with a thrust of his hands on the wheel. No. Already his left arm ached from use and the hand began to float in its own quite isolated climate. At a garage, large, lighted as a night club, he drew up. The young Frenchman he questioned about rooms ran oil-covered fingers through his hair, leaving a dark mark like a brand upon his forehead. He could phone and ask, he said. As the young man phoned John gazed at the main street. Low hanging lights gathered it in patches to form and shape, released it again to darkness and the feeling of leaves. As far as he could see, the garage alone was bright. There was no challenge here. He must stay.

The Frenchman's voice sounded suddenly loud and reassuring. 'Non, non. Il est très gentil. Très gentil.'

John realized the man was speaking of him. To someone he had never met he presented a menace. He, John, in his airforce blazer and grey slacks with his damaged arm and bright pink hand.

The Frenchman returned, grinning, nodding, went with him to the car and pointed his finger into the darkness. A great relief enfolded John. He need go no further. He could sleep. He could lie down near trees. He knew at once that he was very tired. And already he saw the room – the country room of his childhood. Bare boards, washbasin and pitcher. Slop pail. A window close to the trees.

The woman who opened the door to him stood no higher than the crest on his pocket – dress colourless from many washings, hair colourless from neglect. They stood facing each other in the doorway and he was more at ease than she. She was still afraid.

She stepped back though to let him enter, talked quickly then while she handed him the book and waited for him to sign. He glanced at the names and dates above and saw that he would be alone in the small hotel. He signed his name as she talked, taking his time.

'Before the war, all the time we were busy. Many, many people stayed here all the time. But the business has gone off and now, tonight ...'

He barely heard her. And he made no answer. She spoke to release her nervousness. There was no need for him to speak.

She ran up the stairs ahead of him, stopped, beckoning him up. 'The room is not ready but – one minute, one minute only.' She grabbed his bag with violence as if she wrested a weapon from his hand and ran on again, leading him through a dimly lighted upper hallway with bamboo chairs.

The little room was not as he had seen it but it did look out onto trees – dark masses of leaves and the sound of wind. He stood in the room as she made up the bed, her ridiculously short arms smoothing and stretching, her short legs carrying her quickly from one side to the other.

She ran ahead of him to the bathroom, showing him the way. There she scrubbed and flicked a spotlessly clean basin. He put out his good hand to stop her and she drew away as if burned. So she was still frightened. Very frightened. But would discussing it help her? Were he to say, 'I won't hurt you,' would it help? He thought not. But he must give her some reassurance. Outside he said, 'Goodnight, madam – you have taken very good care of me. I am grateful.'

Now he sat on the edge of his bed and found it hard. He took off his shoes without bending down, shoving them off with his toes, gazing about him as he did so. The room was very small: a bureau, a wicker table, a bed. That was all. And down the hall from him, probably locked in her room, was his landlady. Why had she taken him in? Why had she not said she was full up? A store adjoined the hotel downstairs and presumably she had existed on it during the war years. Why then, tonight, was it necessary for her to make two dollars? A dozen reasons revolved in his head, followed immediately by one he felt was correct: she needed the experience of change. He remembered the sentence attributed to him as a child, 'I'd sooner be frightened to death than bored to death.' There were periods in one's life when that was true enough and others – like parts of the war for instance – when the idea of boredom seemed as sweet as a meadow.

He had wiggled his socks off with his toes by now – a trick he'd got into while convalescing. 'Don't favour your arm,' they had said to him. 'You must learn not to favour it.' But that was exactly what he did do. The word had horrified him at first, but he had grown to understand it, grown to know its correctness. Despite all their admonitions, he would 'favour' it for many years. He removed his blazer and shirt and examined the arm minutely. Not a pretty sight. Quite horrible still, in fact – but he favoured it. He laughed aloud as he stood and stepped out of his trousers.

Then he thought about the woman again and it even crossed his mind that if his guess were true, perhaps he owed it to her to give her a fright. Not a serious one, of course, but something she could talk about afterwards, something which would, for a time, raise her stock among the villagers. It was a pleasant kind of fantasy to indulge in but sleep was gradually overtaking him. The wind in the leaves was a soporific. He switched out the light by the door. The room shrank suddenly with darkness and he walked as if in a straitjacket to the bed and lay down. It was good to be lying there, away from the city. He wondered if the woman was asleep. And he slept.

Throughout the night he kept hurting his arm. Pinned between his body and the hard mattress, it would ache and throb and lurch him awake. He imagined himself in the hospital again and listened for the noises of the ward, then slowly the realization of where he was returned to him. Not in a hospital; not in a city. A small place where there were fewer people to stare. And he would sleep again and awaken hurt, reassure himself, hear the movement of leaves and, once, the sound of feet running on earth – a sound that formed a pattern behind his eyes. But later, towards morning, he walked in a meadow and out through a gate and met himself walking in and the old panic gripped him and he greeted himself with so loud a scream that even when it had wakened him it had not quite completed its length and he heard it still – terrible, like a beast in pain.

And then, very wonderfully, came an answering scream: high, shrill, female. As if he had called to a mate and she had replied with immediate urgency. The sound reached him and fulfilled him and he fell asleep then as easily and completely as if he had had a woman.

Not until the sun burst full upon his face did he waken. And he wakened full of the woman, wanting to see her. For now the idea of her answering scream seemed fantastic to him. If he could see her at once, without delay, he would know.

There were no sounds in the hotel as he dressed. The corridor had a sleeping look – forgotten, abandoned. The bamboo chairs cluttered the upstairs hall. Downstairs the room was bare, shabby and empty. No sign of the woman.

He re-climbed the stairs again in search of her and the half dozen doors stared mutely in his face. He began knocking on each in turn and as he returned from their silence she emerged from the first he had tried – her face still blurred with sleep, her hands grown woolly overnight fumbling, fumbling with the fastening at her neck.

He knew nothing from her face and he couldn't ask the question. He said, instead, 'I would like to pay for my room.' And as he extracted the money from his wallet her expression altered. He felt her small eyes hook and sharpen on his favoured hand.

(1947)

Mme Bourgé Dreams of *Brésil*

I s it the hot wet air that lies like a sheet on Paris, or the *confiture de Brésil* in its little pot, placed by *l'inspecteur* on her bedside table? Whatever the reason, Mme Bourgé sleeps a tropical sleep, casting aside a tumble of ecru lace, her torso glistening white as magnolia soap.

Marmoset faces form and shift in the reflecting crystals of chandeliers; glittering jewelled macaws peer from sconces.

Mme Bourgé walks in the black-green jungle, calling, calling. Who is loosed and lost among unfamiliar trees, odours of tree-moss, scents of Shameless Mary? Is it Mme Bourgé herself, now pocked with shadows, trailing leaves and the conjugations of Portuguese verbs?

Marmosets swing in the branches, chatter and wheeze, their faces the size of her thumb's top joint. In their eyes she sees the points of their tiny dreams. Brilliant and noisy as silk umbrellas opening, vast birds rise from her feet.

Za Za is secretive, busy with *macumba*. She models discarded lovers – waxen homunculi jabbed full of pins – forgetful now of their shapes, their given names. In a day, in a week, their beautiful strength will fail them. Mme Bourgé scolds, 'Oh, heartless, heartless Za Za, leaving the pin box empty, the candle guttering wax.'

Late afternoon sun fills the *sala* with zebras, casts palm-frond stripes on sofas and chairs. Tree orchids split the baroque legs of tables, erupt in delicate durable blooms.

Green light stains the white octagonal tiles of the *copa*, stains Augusto's hornet jacket, his lifted hands. Augusto, coffee maker to the Pretender, wears the royal coat of arms on his golden sleeve. Water, metallic, furious as quicksilver, falls through the green air like a school of trout; is caught in a flannel funnel, a vertical windsock, as if in a landing net. 'Like molten lead plummeting down shot-towers, it is the length of the fall that counts' ... Augusto is offering some simple lesson, but Mme Bourgé is falling too. 'When or where?' she cries, and 'where or when?' But Augusto, nimble, bearing a polished tray with pie-crust edging, pours her a *cafézinho* black as tar.

Still half asleep in the stifling morning, Mme Bourgé stretches a lazy arm. Into the pale trumpet of the house phone she calls Augusto. 'A windsock for the equatorial winds,' she sighs, 'and little suits for the marmosets – of satin.'

How can she grasp an air that has no hand-holds, cling to this curve of space? Mme Bourgé waits, ear pressed to the receiver, for the reassurance of Augusto's voice.

(1987)

The Glass Box

t eight forty-five exactly the phone rang and she caught it after the first ring.

The voice said quietly, 'Ricky?'

'Yes.'

'Tonight?'

'Yes. Where?'

'There?'

'Okay.' She glanced about her as she spoke. 'When?'

'Between nine-thirty and nine forty-five.'

She was silent a moment.

'Isn't that all right? I can't be more definite.'

'That's all right.' Her left hand clenched in the pocket of her housecoat. 'Goodbye.'

'Goodbye ...'

She walked back to her room along the hall, quietly past Billie's door for fear he was in and would call her. She thought back over the conversation on the phone, dividing it into two parallel columns in her mind: what had been heard here? what at the other end? A vague fear gathered about her, increased. She had not said enough, not been sufficiently chatty. She shouldn't have dropped her voice or made it so toneless. She shouldn't have been so close to the phone when it rang. As always this worry was like the soft mouth of a fish nuzzling at her physical outline.

There was no time to settle to anything and no inclination to settle. She drew the blind more carefully and tidied the room for the second time, moving on legs that seemed to have ramrods jammed down them, her hands frozen and streaming with perspiration like hands sculptured from ice and now slowly melting. Her face looked too tense in the mirror as she dressed, and too white. Staring at herself she felt suddenly that everything she tried to hide was written all over her for everyone to read. But behind this layer of thought lay another – a layer in which her mind was active and accurate: she had better be ready before nine-thirty in case he was early, better meet him outside to prevent his ringing the bell.

She slipped a dress off its hanger and pulled it over her head, thrusting her fingers under the weight of hair caught in the neckline, tossing it out so that it fell down heavy and thick on her shoulders. The clock said 9:05. She put on her overshoes and threw her fur coat on the bed. If she met anyone on the way out she ought to have some fairly obvious reason for going – something self-evident, like a letter in her hand. Quickly she extracted a bill from the papers on her desk, wrote a cheque to cover it and addressed the envelope. She took a cigarette from the box and lit it, the fat white tube making her lips project. Unmoving, unreal as a store dummy, she drew the smoke deeply into her lungs. There was silence in the boarding house and the room ready.

Just after nine-fifteen she let herself out of the front door and paused a minute on the snowy steps. The strong rays of the street lamp lit her too clearly, fell with a flat violence on the white envelope in her hand. She thrust it into her pocket so that no one, seeing her, would presume she was walking towards the pillar box. Coat collar high about her ears, she turned right on the sidewalk, her overshoes making a crisp squeaking noise on the hard-packed snow. When she reached the corner she stopped in the shadow of a tree, pivoting slightly. An oblique glance at Miss Armitage's window showed a line of yellow outlining the blinds. Miss Armitage was in. Better to know for certain than not know. They would have to come in quietly then, trusting they would not be heard, trusting they would meet no one. If they were, if they did, she would have to break into conversation easily and in that case she had better plan now what she would say.

A group of people rounded the far corner coming towards her. She crossed the street casually to avoid them, stood in front of a shop window, examined minutely the crepe paper decorations and the welter of cheap articles for sale. She was directly opposite the boarding house. If Miss Armitage raised her blind she could see her. Casually again, she moved on to a patch of shadow cast by the Masonic Temple, her eyes sweeping the street from left to right. Great mounds of snow glistened softly in the light and faded grey-white, blue-white, in the shadows, sprang glistening and white again beneath the further lights and so on, here, there, for miles throughout the city.

Then she saw him. He rounded the corner by the tree, head down against the cold. He was walking briskly, intently, as if hurrying to work. His shoulders jutted black and square against the snow. She crossed the street again, planning the point where they would meet – a point at which Miss Armitage, if she did raise the blind, would be unable to see them. She hurried across the slippery road and climbed over the snow bank and the snow filled the tops of her overshoes and settled round her ankles. He didn't alter his pace when he saw her and she fell in beside him.

'Hello,' he said. The crook of his elbow nudged against her ribs.

'Hello.'

They walked together along the sidewalk and up the steps and she turned the key in the lock and they went upstairs. As they reached the landing Miss Armitage called, 'Is that you, Mr Hopper?'

Her heart set up a racket as she called back, 'No, it's only me.'

Miss Armitage said, 'Oh, I thought it was Mr Hopper. That girlfriend of his has been phoning again.'

She led the way along the corridor and he watched her footsteps, treading when she did. He put out a hand and touched her shoulder and she jumped under the contact and didn't turn. When he was inside her room and the door closed, she leaned back against it, trembling. Her head and shoulders and the palms of her hands were flat against the wood. The soft grey fur of her coat moved and fluttered gently with her breathing. She felt like a moth impaled in a collector's show case.

'Cold?' he asked and she shook her head. 'Not only cold.'

He ran his hands beneath her coat, holding his fingers widespread across her back. He pulled her away from the door, let his head drop so that his face was hidden between the fur and her neck. His breath was warm against her cold skin. But above the slight movements of her body, above the sound of his breath and hers, his blood and hers, she listened closely, her flesh a sounding board.

He slid his hands over her shoulders to take off her coat and she stood there, unassisting and still tense. He walked her backwards and pushed her onto the bed and bent to undo her overshoes. When he pulled, her shoes came off too, and she sat there in her stocking feet with the dark bands around her ankles where the snow had melted. He ran his fingers up the silk of her stockings and cupped his palms over her bent knees and she saw him for the first time and noticed the small lines about his eyes, dark, as if drawn with a mapping pen. She lifted her hand to his face and the fingers of it shook and twitched uncontrollably.

A tableau, the two of them, under the ceiling light, with the walls closing in upon them like a box and the walls glass. Difficult to speak now, difficult to laugh or argue or fool as they once had. Three hours together and they wore the time like chains. Imprisoned by it the minutes went clanking by. The world loved lovers only when they didn't love. Kiss on a street-corner and the police told you to hurry along. Take a hotel room and the detective asked you for your marriage licence. Thou shalt not commit adultery. Fat chance.

Urgently she got up, reached for his coat, bearing the heavy weight of it with him a moment before he released it, holding it briefly alone.

'Darling, I ...' The silence came down like a gag.

'Go on.'

She dropped the coat on the chair and put her arms around his neck. 'It's just that we never have long enough, do we?'

'Perhaps, one day.' He looked uneasily about the room and back to her again, his eyes lighting as if they had found what they sought. He picked her up and carried her to the bed, laid her down gently and she stared up at him. Her face looked pale and stiff and transparent like freshly ironed white organdy.

'Don't look at me like that. Oh, Ricky, it's not my fault.'

'I know, darling.'

He threw his jacket on the chair and fell on the bed face downward, his mouth seeking hers.

A bell rang and she jumped like a fish and then froze, her hands rigid on his back. She heard the rattle of Miss Armitage's mules going down the stairs, the front door opening. She strained every nerve listening and the silence was hard and solid like concrete in her ears. Then the rattle of the mules again on the stairs and she sat bolt upright and he vaulted clear of the bed. The sound of her heart was so loud it should have blocked out all noise, but she heard clearly the mounting staccato of the mules continuing along the corridor. As if there were no dimension to time and everything was happening simultaneously, she put on lipstick, combed her hair, noted that he was sitting on the chair, that the coats were, somehow, now on the bed. She felt as if she was taking shorthand at two hundred words a minute and hoping to intercept Miss Armitage, she went down the corridor, walked as far as Miss Benson's door, saying like an automaton, 'Anything for me?'

'A wire.'

'For *me?*'

Miss Armitage leaned against the wall, clearly intending to stay until the message was read. Ricky's fingers shook as she opened the gummed flap. 'Happy birthday darling wonder what you are doing and if you are happy stop have just drunk your health in Johnny Begg love the family.' She heard her mother's gently inquisitive affectionate voice behind the words. She laughed at the stupid family joke about Johnny Begg and handed the telegram to Miss Armitage who said, 'Many happy returns. You should have told us it was your birthday, we'd have had a cake.' Then after a slight pause, 'Say, you can't sit there in your room like that. I'll see if I can find a game of bridge.'

'No, no, please. I brought back work from the office.' She had spoken too quickly. 'It's awfully good of you but I've got to get this work cleared up.'

Miss Armitage surveyed her critically, produced a pack of cigarettes from her pocket and said, 'You do a lot of work for a young girl. Why don't you get yourself a boyfriend like anyone else your age?' She tapped the cigarette on her thumbnail and said, 'Match?'

'I'll get one.'

Miss Armitage followed her. She tried to will Miss Armitage to stop. 'My room's in an awful mess. Really awful. I'd much sooner you didn't see it. You'd give me my marching orders if you did. And rooms are so hard to get these days.' She bantered, giggled, wondering how she would finally stop her if Miss Armitage insisted upon coming in.

Miraculously the telephone rang. The sharp peal of its bell released the balloons of her lungs.

'This place!' Miss Armitage wailed and clattered away.

Ricky ran into the bedroom. 'You've got to hide,' she whispered and as she spoke she was pulling the clothes along in her cupboard to make room, taking his coat and hat and rubbers and stashing them away.

'I won't be long, I swear. But don't move until I say your name.' He obeyed her. She picked up some matches and went along the hall, meeting Miss Armitage just as she turned the corner.

'For Mr Hopper again. That girl sure is after him.'

'Your match.' Ricky was afraid of a long detailed account of the love lives of the various boarders. Feeling hedged into a small space, attempting to appear unhurried, she dreaded every minute the appearance of someone else in the hall; someone else to delay her. Her hand shook again as she held the match and the flame seemed to bounce and jerk about. She wondered why Miss Armitage said nothing.

Miss Armitage took a deep drag of the smoke and held the cigarette loosely in the flabby corner of her mouth. 'If I was your mother,' Miss Armitage began, took out the cigarette and removed a piece of tobacco from her lip, 'I'd see to it you led a different life,' Miss Armitage said. Miss Armitage's bulk blocked all exits. Enclosed by Miss Armitage, Ricky was trapped. She wondered what Miss Armitage meant, what Miss Armitage knew. She fought for words to release her, forced them through the tightness of her throat and heard herself saying jokingly, conversationally, 'But you aren't, are you?' The exits opened again. Miss Armitage was standing in the hall, quite normally life size – a rather tired landlady smoking a cigarette. Ricky patted her arm warmly and smiled. 'I'd better return to my unhealthy pursuits. Goodnight.'

She walked easily to the corridor in the way she had taught herself but once round the corner her body began twitching and her head jerking strangely on her neck. She tensed her muscles to control it and said, 'Stop it, you fool!' consciously once, only to find herself repeating, 'You fool, you fool,' over and over again, unable to stop. She tried to make herself think what to do next but the words of the telegram raced through her head. Hope you are happy. Happy! Silly conventional, unreal language. She was suddenly furious with her family.

She opened her bedroom door and stood still a minute before calling him. He emerged looking slightly absurd, his hair disordered and hanging over his forehead in curly bangs. He was clowning a bit about the stiffness of his knees. His laughter made fury snap in her and her face contorted with tears. She turned her back on him and walked away. Sobs started from an unbelievable depth, broke and left her with a rarefied sensation in the top of her head as if oxygen was being released beneath her skull.

He went up behind her, wrapped his arms round her, rocked her gently from side to side, held his head close to hers saying, 'Darling, darling, what is it?'

The fury abated a little. A kind of tolerant contempt replaced it.

'You don't know?' Her voice was chipped. He didn't answer.

'All right, I'll tell you. I just can't take it any longer, that's all. Nothing more complicated than that. For months and months I've done nothing that's spontaneous. Every move mapped out; everyone a spy or a potential spy. Oh Christ! can't you see? Every doorbell, every telephone, every voice in the hall.' She covered her face with her hands, shuddering.

'Oh, take me out of here,' she said and she brushed past him, pulled a blanket from the bed, began tugging at her over-shoes.

'She can't find you here or know that you've been – that anyone's been. Can't you see that?' She tied her laces in garbled sorts of knots. 'We've got to take a risk – go down the back stairs and through the kitchen. If the maids are still there or if

114

… No, you'll have to go that way. If Armitage hears anything she'll be out like a shot. I'll have to go the front way and cover the noise you make.'

She was getting into her coat with fierce jerking movements and he stood looking at her in amazement. She was trying to think what reason she could give if she were confronted. Lies, lies, she thought. It'll be unnatural to be honest again. She was impatient as he kicked his feet into his rubbers.

'You take this,' she thrust the blanket at him, 'and this,' she fumbled in a drawer for a flashlight. 'The lights go on at the foot of the stairs.' She glanced quickly along the passage and then pushed him through the door. 'Be quick unless you hear my voice. If you do, stay in the back hall until I've stopped talking.'

Overshoes muffling her footsteps she started out again. Thrusting her hands in her pockets she came across the envelope she had taken with her before. She wondered if the maids had gone, if he was OK in the kitchen. She was furious and humiliated by the deceits and camouflages which had accompanied their relationship from the beginning.

Miss Armitage did not appear. Her bedroom door, opening onto the well of the stairs, was so strategically placed that bad luck alone prevented her from seeing all exits and entrances.

Ricky went down the stairs leaning her weight on the banister so that the floorboards wouldn't creak. Black silence filled the place.

He was not there when she reached the main floor and, instinctively, habitually, she went to the sitting room window and searched the still, snowy street. Re-entering the hall, she saw him. Together, as ghosts might fall into step, they walked to the door. Unspeaking, they moved without conscious awareness of each other as two bird dogs behave identically and independently when concerned with the same bird. The door's closing joined them again and for a split second they looked into each other's eyes and smiled. The fierceness of the cold sprang at them, stinging. When they opened their mouths to speak it filled their throats. She noticed his nervous glance about as they walked; the crunch of their heels, sounding like breaking glass, startlingly loud; and his face, white, as if a handkerchief had been tied across it, below the shadow cast by his hat.

Rounding the corner she saw with relief that the frost had made the windows of his car opaque. Even the cold was easier to fight than the long light summer evenings with the glass of the windows clear. The car doors banged, once, twice, against the city.

'My darling.' He leaned across to her, knocking the gear shift out of the way with his elbow as he did so. 'My very own dear.'

But the sense of security vanished again as he kissed her. Perhaps the car had been there too long and someone had seen it. Any one of a dozen people might have recognized it and wondered why it was there. She felt the nervousness growing in him as it did in herself. Pitiful security – frost on panes of glass. He pulled away from her then and started the engine, thawed out the front panel so he could see. 'We'd better move on, just to be on the safe side.'

He engaged the engine and they pulled out into the street, the chains on the wheels rattling a little and clanking.

(1943)

George

All of us in the boarding house were pretty much relieved when George came. We had had, earlier, a succession of houseboys, each worse than the one before. Then there had been a long period with no one. So that night at dinner, when Ladlaw drew George out of her hat like a rabbit everybody felt a good deal happier. Already Ladlaw herself was grinning. He had come that morning, she said, and worked hard all day. A few sceptical eyebrows were raised. We had heard her eulogies before. His references were OK, he'd worked at an army camp and likely knew what discipline meant, she figured.

Ernie Arnold suggested we place side bets on George. He began drawing columns on the back of his menu.

'I'll bet anyone a bottle of beer that within a week he's raided my cellar,' Mr Jackson volunteered. Mr Jackson was the oldest boarder in all senses. He was also the most affluent.

'There's nobody fool enough to take that,' said Mr Cooms. 'You've only got to win to lose.'

Miss Kirtle was smiling and nodding and looking bright and hovering on the brink of speech.

'Come,' said Mr Jackson chidingly. 'Miss Kirtle will take me up, won't you, Miss Kirtle?'

She crumbled her roll between her fingers, torn between being a good sport and involving herself in betting.

Ernie was very busy. I leaned over to watch him. Down the left-hand edge of the paper he had written our names. He was chuckling to himself. Across the top were various headings: Just Plain Lazy; Kleptomaniac; Dipsomaniac; Religious Maniac; How Long He'll Stay.

'Now, look,' he said. 'Opposite your own name you put a tick in the columns you think apply, filling in the final column with the number of days you think he'll stay. Then everyone puts a dollar in the kitty.'

'And if everyone ticks the same column?' I said.

'Now, wait. I've got this all figured out. Leave it to Ernie. If everyone ticks the same column, then everyone gets some of their money back – the amount depending on how many ticks they have that are false and how close they come to guessing the number of days he stays.'

'It all sounds pretty complicated to me,' I said, 'but if you want to figure it out, that's your business.' He was not listening to me by this time but had taken my menu and was busy at work again.

'Ernie's working out a fancy kind of sweepstake,' I said, and I explained.

'What happens to the money if George is a complete success?'

Ernie looked up from his writing. 'I've got it all figured,' he said. 'If George turns out to be a paragon, we give the money to him.'

'Oh!' said Miss Kirtle, disappointed.

'This is one hell of a sweepstake,' said Mr Cooms.

'You don't have to play, you know,' said Ernie. 'Only those as wishes. You'll come in?' he said to me.

'Sure.'

'And you, Miss Ladlaw?'

'What I want to know,' she said, 'is why you had to write all over my menus?'

'Emergency,' said Ernie.

But Miss Ladlaw was in a good mood that night.

'There's just one thing,' I said. 'No one must encourage George to develop the characteristics they've ticked. For instance, if you bet he's a kleptomaniac, you mustn't tempt him. It looks to me as if we might make him what we want him to be and be in a couple of dollars and out a houseboy.'

'That,' said Ernie, 'is in the rules.' And he read.

'What I'm curious about,' Mr Jackson interrupted, 'is who holds the money meanwhile? Being the oldest and most respectable among you I think I should.'

'I've thought of all that too,' said Ernie. 'The money and the betting chart are to be placed in a sealed envelope and put in the cash box. But here, I'll pass you the rules and the chart and you can read for yourself and place your bets at the same time.'

Miss Ladlaw raised a few objections at first and then began to laugh and awkwardly walked out to the cash box in the hall desk and returned with her dollar.

There was a great deal of consultation and chat before the chart was finally filled. Miss Kirtle was worried and anxious and timid but Mr Jackson persuaded her it was all just fun. She told me afterwards she'd ticked Religious Maniac as it was the only *nice* thing on the list but that she couldn't think how long he'd stay. She talked about this for some time afterwards. 'My dear, when I came to the column about how long he'd stay, I just couldn't *think*.'

Miss Ladlaw ticked every column and gave his duration of service as two weeks, explaining that if she lost a houseboy she'd at least have some money back. Ernie pointed out that he'd have to have all the faults listed before she'd get much back and she muttered, suddenly lugubrious and grim, that she expected he had and more besides.

All the boarders but Mr Coxton anted up. He said, 'No thank you,' and went on reading his newspaper.

That made seven dollars from the house. Then five of the 'regulars' who came in from nearby rooming-houses asked if they could join in too. They felt they ought to get a different rate as they would have to take our word for George's behaviour, but we talked them out of that and Ernie promised if George got drunk he'd phone them up, no matter what time, so they could come and see for themselves. So, altogether, there was an even twelve dollars in the kitty which was duly sealed in the presence of all and put in the cash box in the desk.

That was a Friday night. I don't think any of us saw George on our way to work in the morning. I didn't, anyway, but a deep snow had fallen overnight and as I opened the front door I saw the steps had been carefully shovelled and brushed. If he was Just Plain Lazy, there was no evidence yet. I felt a bit mean about George as I walked to work. If a whole houseful of persons expects the worst of a guy and almost perversely hopes it, what chance has he got? But letting my mind run backwards over his predecessors, I felt perhaps we were justified.

I came home well after the lunch hour that afternoon. There on the step in khaki drill slacks and shirt, wearing a green eye-shade, was, presumably, George. He was polishing the brass on the front door. He was very small, very thin, like a bird and had quick movements. No, not Just Plain Lazy, I judged. Not with that build.

'Hello,' I said as I came up to him. 'Aren't you cold without a coat?' He jumped at my words. His dark-skinned face twitched, he twisted his mouth from side to side, touched his hand to his eye-shade.

'Good afternoon, miss,' he said and reached out and opened the door for me – oh, so obsequious, so squirming.

So that, I thought, is George, and I couldn't help laughing. As I went upstairs I visualized the twelve dollars being handed over to him.

Rita Ferguson was in her room as I passed. I poked my head in. 'Have you seen our monster?' I asked.

She looked up from her nails, holding an emery board at an angle. 'Not yet. Have you?'

I nodded.

'What's he like?'

'You wait and see. Heaven knows what we're in for now!'

'Well, he can clean, anyway,' she said. 'The baseboard in my room's been dusted for the first time since I arrived.'

'How do you know?'

'I tried it with my finger when I came in. I always do.'

'And let the dust accumulate?'

'Why not? God knows I pay enough for service.'

'Well, you've got it now, but don't be surprised if you're visited some dark night.' I went on to my room. A few minutes later Rita was leaning against the frame of my door. She was still filing her nails.

'Tell me the truth,' she said. 'Is he really that bad?'

'You wait and see,' I said ominously.

'Well, I think it's disgraceful there are no keys to our doors I've always thought it was. I'm going out and get a locksmith and have one made today.'

'Don't be too hasty,' I said, 'wait and see. He may be your type.'

'You're not a bit funny,' she flared up. 'Not a bit,' and she left. Rita, I thought, is a good careful girl and her family need never worry about her.

I was out to dinner that night so wasn't there for the grand note-comparing that took place in the dining-room. I was told later that Rita had been very angry with me when she got an accurate description of George and that spirits were considerably lower than they had been the night before, and that Miss Kirtle was so distressed about her dollar bet now that she'd seen the man that they had had to give it her back, she'd fretted so. Miss Ladlaw's report was that, so far, he'd worked 'pretty good', and that was high praise from her.

But I knew none of that until next day and after my second encounter with George. I was wakened on the Sunday morning by a tap on my door and a second later the door was pushed open to disclose George, his white jacket making a light smudge in the dark.

'Oh, good morning, George,' I said. 'Come in,' and I stretched for the light switch and smoothed a place on the bed. He stood there, confused, the white jacket almost swamping him, holding the tray as if it was a baby and he so unused to them, too. He was terribly embarrassed, really acutely so. He didn't dare look anywhere but at the tray and he seemed unable to move. At last, with a great effort he walked quickly, jerkily, across the floor, deposited the tray like a robot and fled from the room on rubber-soled shoes.

Well, I thought, looking at my watch comfortably, he evidently doesn't have to go to early service. I tried to think of his face and couldn't. It was dark-skinned, thin and twitching but his eye-shade hid the upper half with shadow and it was impossible to guess what it was really like. Impossible to imagine it had ever been seen close up, as a barber might see it or a woman who loved him, but he hasn't got a hangover, I reflected as I began my grapefruit, and he doesn't go to early service. Two very good points.

Talk of George had dwindled considerably by Monday. Everyone chivvied everyone else a little over the sweepstake and it was generally conceded that George would get the eleven dollars and deserve it, too. And as the days wore on and the house remained beautifully warm and the snow was beautifully shovelled and the brass beautifully shined, we all felt a little small for having been so suspicious. At last we didn't feel anything about it any more, but took our comforts for granted and went on as usual, Miss Ferguson, however, had a key made for her door.

It was two weeks to the day since George's arrival when I was sitting in the hall after dinner and listening to Ernie telling me about his plans for skiing that weekend at St Sauveur. 'I'm going to learn to christie if I rupture myself,' he said.

Suddenly there was a mass exodus from the dining room – all the old girls with the feather hats and pearls and their impeccably tailored husbands who came in frequently from neighbouring apartments. At the same moment the front door opened and there was George, bowing his way through the diners, his left hand lifting his bowler hat to the ladies, his right raised in a V for Victory salute. A carnation shone from his button-hole. He wore grey gloves and spats.

'A beautiful evening,' he said, bowing and smiling. 'How nice to see everyone,' he said. 'But you must excuse me, I can't stay to talk,' and he moved on down the hall, while behind him, receiving small encouraging phrases like, 'That's right, Tom,' came a liveried man carrying a parcel. George stepped aside when he reached the cellar door while Tom opened it for him, then he disappeared from sight with Tom following.

'Well!' said Ernie. 'The future is looking up,' he said.

Ladlaw came into the hall from the kitchen and we told her about it. Ernie acted it out and was very funny.

'I don't believe it,' said Ladlaw. 'Why, that guy's too shy to speak.'

'Not tonight, he isn't,' I replied and at that point Tom emerged from the cellar and marched to the front door.

'Who was that?' asked Ladlaw.

'That,' said Ernie, 'is George's retainer. The one we told you about. Remember?'

When Ernie told the news to the dining room Miss Kirtle was pretty upset she'd taken her dollar back and Rita smiled in a mean way and I knew she was thinking about her key.

Nothing more happened that night and next day everything was in order. Ernie said, 'He's got a split personality, I guess, and it sure is split. As long as he doesn't get the two halves mixed, we're okay.' But that night, after dinner, just as everyone was leaving, the same thing happened again. In swept George, complete with carnation and spats, his bowler hat raised as before, bowing and smiling for all the world like royalty condescending to the populace. This time, however, he stopped at the desk where Ladlaw was sitting. 'Good evening,' he said and his patronizing air had reached its peak. But before he could go further Ladlaw spoke up in an ugly voice.

'You get down to your room and no more of this.'

'Me?' said George, only you couldn't think of him as George any more. 'Me?' and he struck a preposterous attitude of wounded dignity. 'How dare you speak to me that way?' And he bent right over the desk and glared into Ladlaw's face very close and menacing.

She put her hand on his shoulder and pushed him, 'Now get downstairs,' she said. 'Pronto!'

'Poor soul,' he said suddenly and smiling sweetly. 'Poor, poor soul!' and then, 'Come, Tom, this way,' and he went to the basement door, waited for Tom to open it, and disappeared from sight.

By now we were all chattering and excited over the two Georges. Mr Jackson even suggested the sweepstake wasn't fair any more – that we'd placed our bets on the houseboy and it had turned out there were two of them. How was Ernie going to figure it out now? But Ernie, presumably, was figuring out christies at St Sauveur.

'Nobody's going to win that money, anyway,' said Mr Cooms. 'George doesn't suffer from any of the complaints we ticked, he has a whole new set of his own.' Miss Kirtle smiled happily. 'It will depend now on who guessed closest how long he'll stay.'

'Oh, dear, and I just couldn't think,' said Miss Kirtle.

'Never mind,' said Mr Cooms roughly, 'you're not in the running any more.'

I was out again that evening and didn't get back till late. I was tired when I put the key in the door and I noticed by the desk clock it was after twelve-thirty. As I turned to go up the stairs there was Ladlaw sitting on the top step. Her hair was up in curlers and she was in her dressing gown.

'Are you any good with drunks?' she asked.

'Why?'

She pointed downstairs and said, 'Listen.'

I listened. 'I don't hear anything,' I said.

'Wait.'

The house was completely still. I could hear the clock ticking on the desk. In the distance a car horn sounded, somebody laughed on the street and then I jumped nearly out of my skin. A radio had been turned on full blast so it practically shook the house. I waited for it to be turned down a bit so it would be easier to speak and I sat down on the step beside Ladlaw. But it wasn't turned down. Instead, it was followed by an extraordinary banging and bumping.

'What's he doing?'

Ladlaw shook her head wearily. 'It's been going on like this ever since ten-thirty. I can't get him to stop.'

'Is there anyone in?'

'Only Miss Kirtle who's scared to death and Miss Ferguson who's locked her door.'

'I'll go down,' I said, not wanting to. 'I'll see what I can do.'

When I opened the cellar door the noise came at me solid. You had to fight against it. I couldn't imagine what I'd do once I got there – why I was going down those stairs. When I got to the bottom George's door was shut, the banging and bumping had stopped but the radio hadn't. I knocked. No answer. I knocked again with my signet ring. No answer.

'George,' I yelled. 'George!' Still no answer, so I opened the door of his room and looked in.

What I had expected to find, I don't know, but what I did find surprised me. The radio, at one side of the room, was on full. The rest of the room was in perfect order. In the centre under a strong white light was a table with great piles of paper on it, all neatly stacked, as business-like as the desk of an executive. Behind it, in his khaki drill, wearing his eye-shade, sat George.

'George,' I said and went across the room to him. He leapt to his feet as he saw me, bowed, took my hand, kissed it with a great resounding smack.

He was drunk as a coot.

I went over and turned down his radio. 'I came down to ask you to do me a favour.'

He bowed again. 'Anything, dear,' he said.

'Look,' I said. 'I can't sleep, George. I simply can't sleep with the radio on so loud. Would you turn it down a little?' I still had on my fur coat and my overshoes but he didn't seem to notice.

'At twelve o'clock,' he said, suddenly aggressive and ugly. 'I will at twelve, not before.'

'But it's after twelve now.'

For answer he went and hit the face of the alarm clock with the back of his fingers. It said five past ten.

I felt beaten then. 'Look, George,' I said. 'I want a cup of coffee. How about having one with me if I make it?'

He was domineering, arrogant. 'I want my dinner. Get me my dinner.'

'But you had your dinner earlier.'

'No, I didn't.' He shook his fist in my face and I moved closer to the door. 'Ladlaw,' he said pulling a face, 'wouldn't give me any.'

'I'll get you some,' I said, not stopping to argue. 'Right now,' I said and I was thankful for a reason to leave.

He looked at me very closely and I saw his eyes for the first time and remembered how I had thought about his face before and wondered if anyone had ever seen it close up. They were minute, brown and slightly crossed, which evidently accounted for the eye-shade, and they had an expression in them that scared hell right out of me.

'I'll make you some sandwiches,' I said and I went out of the door as fast as I dared and up the stairs with the terrible care of the pursued who doesn't want the pursuer to know he knows.

Ladlaw was waiting for me when I came up. 'Well?' she asked.

'He says he's hungry and that he won't turn the radio down before twelve.'

'Twelve?' she said.

'Yes. I'm going to get him a meal. It may sober him up.'

We went into the kitchen and I picked up a tray in the pantry en route. Ladlaw went into the cold room and said, 'There's lamb or chicken.'

'Make it chicken,' I said.

She came back and plunked the plate on the table, rinsed some lettuce under the tap. I put the water on for coffee and a slight smell of gas escaped.

'I think you've got a gas leak,' I said, but what I meant was that I didn't want to go down into the basement again. I leaned my hands on top of the percolator a few minutes, thinking. Then I began cutting sandwiches.

I cut those sandwiches as if I were cutting them for a lover. The bread thin with plenty of butter, the chicken in beautiful white slices spread with mayonnaise and then the curling green lettuce. I set the tray as if my life depended on it and waited for the coffee to perk and hoped it never would.

When it was ready I said, 'Coffee?' and Ladlaw nodded. 'Well,' I announced, sitting on the stool at the kitchen table, 'it's all ready,' and I put a couple of lumps of sugar in my cup and began stirring.

Ladlaw nodded at the tray. 'Aren't you going to take it down?'

'I thought you would.'

She shook her head. 'No point in me taking it. I only make

him mad. You'd better go. You said you would. He'll be expecting you.'

'That's just what I'm afraid of,' I said.

We sat there a few minutes. The coffee slipped down warm and soothing. 'All right, I'll go,' I said at last, 'but you've got to come with me. Right behind.'

So we set off down the hall, through the cellar door and down the stairs. We didn't speak. There was nothing to say and we couldn't have heard each other anyway because of the radio. She turned the handle of George's door for me and I pushed in thinking how scared he'd seemed the first Sunday he brought me breakfast and how neatly the tables had been turned.

He was sitting as before, at his table under the white light. He gave me the creeps rather. I wondered what he was doing with all those papers.

'There.' I put the tray down on a table near the door. 'There's a nice meal for you.'

He made a wide gesture of disdain and didn't look at the tray again. As before he leaped to his feet and came forward. He took my hand, kissing it with the inside of his lips.

'You're just like my girlfriend,' he said and his clutch tightened and I saw those dreadful little eyes for the second time.

'Eat your supper, turn down your radio and go to bed.' I pulled away from him and he followed me to the door. 'Remember about the radio, George – for my sake.' I said it sweetly.

He lunged at me, pressed me to him with a dreadful ardour and I saw the hairs growing out of his dark greasy neck. 'Goodnight,' he said. 'My love!'

I started up the stairs quickly to ensure that Ladlaw would be between George and me. At the top I leaned against the wall, shaking and giggling. Ladlaw said, 'Keep going,' and we went on to the kitchen and sat with our elbows on the kitchen table and finished the coffee.

'It all began the day he got paid,' she said. 'He was so good up till then. Sometimes I wonder what's the point of keeping on trying.'

We got up then. I slipped a knife into my pocket as we went. The hall clock said twenty-five to two as we passed.

When I got to my room I took the knife from my pocket and tried it in my door. It held fast. I felt better then and made a face in Rita's direction. I was fearfully tired. I sat on the bed in my coat and lit a cigarette and listened. The radio had been turned down. I undressed and opened the door onto the balcony and plugged it so it wouldn't bang and fixed the knife in the other door and fell into bed. Well, one thing, I thought before I went to sleep – I ticked Dipsomaniac!

I don't know how long I slept but when I wakened it was suddenly. I listened, hearing nothing. As far as I could tell my door was still shut. Then I knew what had wakened me. I was hot. I was so hot that the perspiration was rolling down me. The floor was hot under my feet as I got out of bed. A thaw, I thought, and imagined how mad Ernie would be. I flung my balcony door wide and the air came in like cold steel. No sign of a thaw. I went over to the radiator and the pipes burned me. Something was mighty queer. I put on my dressing gown and slippers and opened my door quietly. There was movement on the landing and whispering. The temperature in the hall was staggering.

I found Ladlaw and Miss Kirtle talking. Miss Kirtle was dead white and her eyes were immense with fear. 'He's set fire to the place,' she said. 'Oh, we'll all be burned to death.' Her lip trembled.

'Go and get dressed,' I said, 'at once. And get your bags packed. Go along.' She went like a child, whimpering a little.

'What goes on?' I asked Ladlaw.

She gave a twisted, terrible smile. 'He's stoking,' she said. 'Must have been for hours. He's standing there stark naked with sweat running down and stoking.'

'Have you told him to stop?'

'He doesn't hear,' she said. 'He doesn't even know I was down. He's just stoking.'

I ran upstairs and knocked on Mr Jackson's door. He didn't answer. I walked in, turned on his light and went over and shook him. 'Mr Jackson,' I called. 'Mr Jackson.' He wakened sleepily.

'Get up,' I said. 'You've got to help us with George.'

He got out of bed hanging onto his pyjama pants with one hand and covering his mouth with the other. Teeth, I thought, and I went into the hall and waited. In a minute he came out, tying his dressing gown cord.

'God,' he said. 'Is it a heat wave?'

'George is stoking. He thinks he's in a ship or something. You must go down.'

I went to the cellar door with him for something to do. I waited. I could hear the shovel going and then Mr Jackson's voice. I waited a long time and then Mr Jackson came upstairs. He was biting his lip and his eyes were focusing on something far away. 'Screwy,' he said, tapping his damp forehead. 'He doesn't hear or see. I've locked the coal cellar and taken the key. That's the last pailful he can get.'

'Meanwhile we can burst into flames any moment from the feel of things.'

'Run off the hot water,' he said, 'or the boiler may explode. And open the windows. I'll waken Cooms and see if we can drag him away by force. He's too strong for me, I tried. And don't go down,' he added. 'Understand?'

It was the very last thing I'd have been likely to do. George clad was bad enough.

The water spat and choked from the taps. It was rusty and scalding. While I was in the kitchen I threw out the old coffee grounds and put some fresh on to perk. I wondered about Miss

Kirtle and thought I'd better go up and see how she was getting on.

She had one bag packed and was standing in the middle of the room, an empty suitcase in front of her and dozens of garments lying about waiting to be pushed in. She looked quite different from the other times I'd seen her. Her hair was all twisted up anyhow and the top of her knitted suit was on back to front.

'Don't worry, Miss Kirtle.' I opened her window. 'Mr Jackson's looking after everything. If I were you I'd just lie down.' I pulled the blankets up on her bed and shook the pillow 'Everything'll be all right,' I said.

The house was pretty full of steam and the heat seemed worse by the time Mr Jackson and Mr Cooms came up again.

'So help me, he was slippery as an eel,' said Mr Cooms 'You couldn't get a grip on him.'

'We locked him in his room,' Mr Jackson added. Then turning to Ladlaw, 'You'll have to give him notice the minute he can hear again.'

'The guy's crazy,' said Mr Cooms.

We were all standing there as the hall clock struck seven.

'Breakfast time,' Ladlaw said and we marched into the kitchen. Now that we had time to think we found it hot and cold and everything at once. The steam was clinging to us and the heat fearful, but near the windows the air rushed in freezing.

Ladlaw began squeezing oranges and was happier busy. Mr Cooms set the kitchen table and Mr Jackson rocked back and forth – heels, toes – near the stove. Every now and then he shook his head and said, 'God!' in a voice full of wonder.

They didn't talk about George much. I think it must have been because he was naked and that made them shy.

'Something's got to be done,' I said. 'We can't go on like this.'

Ladlaw pursed her lips and stirred her coffee noisily. Mr Jackson buttered a piece of toast and cut it in strips. He attempted to look pontifical but his short white hair standing on end rather destroyed the effect.

'The preliminaries,' he said, waving his knife, 'need not be discussed. The events leading up to last night are of no importance. They are trivia,' he said. I tried to interrupt but he wouldn't let me. 'However,' and this he emphasized, 'when a man reaches the point where he no longer has any judgement – where he stands up mother-naked and stokes like that – where he endangers the lives of others – then it is serious. Very.'

'God knows what he's doing now,' Mr Cooms added. We all jumped.

'I've given it my considered opinion,' said Mr Jackson, 'and there seems to me only one thing to do. We must call the police.'

'I think you're right, Jackson. I don't know why we didn't think of it before.' Mr Cooms jumped up and Mr Jackson followed. 'We can't go through another night with him down there.'

'I don't think we can,' said Ladlaw.

But we did!

The police came all right. They filled the hall with navy blue and questions. One kept hitting his leg with his truncheon. They lounged on chairs and seemed interested in nothing. Mr Jackson told them what they wanted to know. Then they all looked at each other, got up at once, asked the way to the basement and clattered down the stairs. We heard them banging on George's door, talking among themselves. Then they trooped up again, said there was nothing they could do, explained it was impossible to evict, that if he had been making a public nuisance of himself outside they could pick him up – but not inside, in his own room. No, they were sorry. If he went out and we liked to phone them they'd do what they could, provided he was disturbing the peace.

'Meanwhile he can set fire to the house and it's no business of yours?'

The one who kept hitting his leg said huffily that they were only doing their duty, that we had no complaint to make now – he was evidently sleeping. And they left.

'Well!' said Ladlaw, but I anticipated her tirade. 'I don't know about anyone else,' I said, 'but I'm going back to bed. Waken me if there's a murder – not unless.'

When I did waken it was afternoon. The house was quiet and the Sunday feeling unmarred by our activities of the night before. Snow was failing in enormous flakes outside. I remembered I'd left my cigarettes in the kitchen and went down for them.

In the front hall, before the mirror, giving himself a final assessment, was George. He was immaculate. He wore his good overcoat, white silk scarf, bowler hat and an ice-box rose was tucked neatly into his buttonhole.

'Good afternoon,' he said with curt condescension, speaking to me through the mirror without turning. And then, 'Brush me off,' he said and he pointed to a clothes brush on the desk. Amazed at us both I obeyed him. He surveyed the job over his shoulder, put his hand in his pocket, jingled his change, pressed a dime in my hand and left.

I suppose it was the stoking, I thought, as I went up the stairs to Ladlaw's room. I couldn't imagine how anyone as drunk as he'd been could even raise his head at three in the afternoon, let alone be walking briskly about as if he'd gone to bed at ten.

Ladlaw and Mr Jackson were playing Gin Rummy in a kind of tired silence when I went in. 'Look,' I said, 'I thought you'd be interested. I've just had another encounter with George,' and I told them about it, throwing the dime on the card table for proof.

'You say he's gone out?' Mr Jackson asked eagerly and he

jumped to his feet exclaiming, 'We'll get him now. I'll phone the police right away.'

'Don't bother,' I said. 'He's sober as a fish. There's not a policeman in town 'd pick him up now.'

I left the two of them with their amazement and after that I had nothing more to do with George. I was invited out for the rest of Sunday and I was glad to go.

The house was quiet when I returned and the only thing that was unusual at all was a note in Ladlaw's handwriting pinned to my pillow: 'If you hear the doorbell in the night, don't answer it. Mr Jackson and me have locked George out. He only has a key to the back door and we bolted it. 'So,' I thought and I went to bed.

I overslept next morning and didn't have any time for talking or breakfast but I noticed the steps were beautifully shovelled and swept, as usual, and wondered who had been the Boy Scout.

At dinner that night the rest of the story broke. Ladlaw was in the kitchen for the first half of the meal and Mr Jackson, Mr Cooms and myself related our portions of yesterday's adventures. There was a good deal of excitement over the betting. Ernie was sore as hell that he'd missed the fun. He smiled, however, when he heard about the drink. 'I ticked Dipso,' he said.

Miss Kirtle was on the verge of speech as she always was, but no one gave her a chance to say anything. Miss Ferguson who'd slept through the excitement and not ticked Dipsomaniac was busy reading a magazine. The 'regulars' wanted a full report and they got it. Mr Jackson told how he and Miss Ladlaw had locked George out – but he guessed George couldn't have intended coming back anyway as no one heard any doorbells.

'But he *did* come back,' said Miss Kirtle nervously. 'He came in through his window.' Blushing and stammering with all eyes on her, Miss Kirtle began her part of the story. 'This morning he was back at work as if nothing had happened. It was just as if we'd dreamed it,' she said, her eyes round with wonder.

Ernie laughed. 'We can't divide the spoils yet, then,' he said. 'We've got to wait until he's gone. That's in the rules.'

Miss Kirtle was trying to speak again but by this time the conversation had been whisked away from her. She plucked my sleeve. 'My dear,' she said, 'I think they'd be interested. He *has* gone.'

'Look,' I yelled, 'if you'd let Miss Kirtle finish.'

But Ladlaw came in at that point. I suppose, in the whole dining room, nobody really cared about George going but Ladlaw. Some of us would come to care, doubtless, when the house was in shambles again and the water gushed cold out of the taps just when we wanted our baths. But now all that mattered was the story and the sweepstake. Eleven dollars for someone, no one quite knew whom. Mr Jackson swore he'd won and wouldn't listen when anyone doubted him. For myself, I felt it depended largely upon the accuracy of Ernie's fractions.

Ladlaw picked up where Miss Kirtle stopped. 'I told him,' she said, and her voice was tired and not a bit excited, 'that was the last time he got drunk in my house. I was going to give him another chance what with labour so hard to get. But I'd no sooner said the word "drunk" than he started jumping up and down like a maniac. He ran down the stairs and up again swinging his arms and screaming. He said he wouldn't work in such a house. "Go then," I said. And he went.' The story ended there. She told it to get it done with. She was tired as a dog, you could see that, and fed up.

'There,' said Mr Cooms. 'I said seventeen days and seventeen days it is. Friday to Friday – seven days ...'

'Eight,' said Ernie

Mr Cooms pursed his lips and figured on the table top with his finger.

'You haven't a chance, anyway,' said Ernie. 'You ticked

Kleptomaniac if I remember rightly and you never bet he'd drink.'

'Go and get the chart,' I said. 'Go on, Ernie. Work it out now. I've got a bill to pay tomorrow and I'd like the money.'

Reluctantly he rose from his table, casting a rueful eye at his plate as he did so. He'd almost reached the door when Ladlaw spoke up.

'Hey,' she said. 'You'd better save your strength. I forgot to tell you. When George went the cash box went too.'

(1946)

The Green Bird

I cannot escape the fascination of doors, the weight of unknown people who drive me into myself and pin me with their personalities. Nor can I resist the desire to be led through shutters, and impaled on strange living-room chairs.

Therefore when Ernest stood very squarely on his feet and said: 'I'm going to call on Mrs Rowan today and I hope you will come,' I said yes. The desire to be trapped by old Mrs Rowan was stronger than any other feeling. Her door was particularly attractive – set solid and dark in her solid, dark house. I had passed by often and seen no sign of life there – no hand at a window, no small movement of the handle of the door.

We rang the bell. A manservant, smiling, white-coated, drew us in, took our coats, showed us into the living room.

'So it is this,' I said to Ernest.

'Beg your pardon?' He crossed his knees carefully, jerked back his neck with the abstracted manner of the public speaker being introduced, leaned his young black head on Mrs Rowan's air.

'It is this,' I said. 'No ash trays,' I said.

'But I don't smoke,' said Ernest.

Mrs Rowan came then. There were dark bands holding a child's face onto a forgotten body. She sat as though she were our guest and we had embarrassed her.

Ernest handled the conversation with an Oriental formality aided by daguerreotype gestures. Mrs Rowan responded to him – a child under grey hair, above the large, loose, shambling torso. She talked of candy and birthday cake. She said she didn't like radios.

I said, 'Music,' and looked about startled as if someone else had said it, suddenly imagining the horror of music sounding in this motionless house.

She said, 'But you do miss hearing famous speakers. I once heard Hitler when I was in a taxi.' She said, 'We will only sit here a little longer and then we will go upstairs, I have an invalid up there who likes to pour tea.'

I felt the sick-room atmosphere in my lungs and my longing to escape was a strong hand pushing me towards it. I imagined the whole upstairs white and dim, with disease crowding out the light.

Mrs Rowan said, 'We will go now,' and we rose, unable to protest had we wished, and followed her up the carpeted stairs and into a front room where a tea-table was set up. There was a large figure in a chair.

'Miss Price, the invalid,' Mrs Rowan said, 'insists on pouring the tea. She likes it. It gives her pleasure.' The figure in the chair moved only her eyes, staring first at Ernest and then at me. Her face was lifeless as a plate. Mrs Rowan continued to talk about her. 'She's been with me a long time,' she said. 'Poor dear.' And then, 'It's quite all right. Her nurse is right next door.' She introduced us. Miss Price sucked in the corners of her mouth and inclined her head slightly with each introduction. The white-coated, grinning man-servant brought in the tea.

'You can pour it now,' said Mrs Rowan, and Miss Price began, slowly, faultlessly, with the corners of her mouth sucked in and her eyes dark and long as seeds. She paid no attention to what we said about sugar and cream. She finished and folded her arms, watched us without expression.

Mrs Rowan passed the cakestand. 'You eat these first,' she said, pointing to the sandwiches; 'These second,' pointing to some cookies; 'and this last,' indicating fruit cake. My cup rattled a little.

I pretended to drink my tea, but felt a nausea – the cup seemed dirty. Ernest leaned back in his chair, said, 'Delicious tea.' Miss Price sat with her arms folded; there was no indication of life except in the glimmer of her seed eyes.

'Dear,' said Mrs Rowan suddenly but without concern 'you haven't poured yourself a cup.'

Miss Price sucked in her mouth, looked down into her lap; her face was hurt.

'No,' I said. 'You must have a cup too.' I laughed by mistake.

Miss Price looked up at me, flicked her eyes at mine with a quick glance of conspiracy and laughed too, in complete silence. Mrs Rowan passed her a cup and she poured her own tea solemnly and folded her arms again.

'Before you go,' Mrs Rowan said, 'I'd like to give you a book – one of mine. Which one would you like?'

'Why,' I said, looking at the cakestand which had never been passed again and stood with all the food untouched but for the two sandwiches Ernest and I had taken, 'Why –' I wondered what I could say. I had no idea she wrote. 'Why,' I said again and desperately, 'I should like most the one you like most.'

Miss Price flicked her eyes at me again and her body heaved with dreadful silent laughter.

'I like them all,' Mrs Rowan said. 'There are some that are written about things that happened in 300 BC and some written about things that happened three minutes ago. I'll get them,' she said, and went.

Ernest was carefully balancing his saucer on his knee, sitting very straight. There was no sound in the entire house.

'I hope you are feeling better, Miss Price,' Ernest said.

I saw the immense silent body heave again, this time with sobs. Dreadful silent sobs. And then it spoke for the first time 'They cut off both my legs three years ago. I'm nothing but a stump.' And the sobbing grew deeper, longer.

I looked at Ernest. I heard my own voice saying, 'Such a

lovely place to live, this – so central. You can see everything from this room. It looks right out on the street. You can see everything.'

Miss Price was still now, her face expressionless, as if it had happened years before. 'Yes,' she said.

'The parades,' I said.

'Yes, the parades. My nephew's in the war.'

'I'm sorry,' Ernest said.

'He was wounded at Ypres. My sister heard last week.' Her arms were folded. Her cup of tea was untouched before her, the cream in a thick scum on the surface.

'Now, here,' Mrs Rowan came in, her arms full of books, like a child behind the weight of flesh – covetous of the books – of the form of the books, spreading them about her, never once opening their covers. 'Which one would you like?' she asked.

'This,' I said. 'The colour of its cover will go with my room'

'What a pretty thought,' Mrs Rowan said, and for some reason my eyes were drawn to Miss Price, knowing they would find her heaving with that silent laughter that turned her eyes to seeds.

'We must go,' said Ernest suddenly. He put down his cup and stood up. I tucked the book under my arm and crossed to Miss Price. 'Goodbye,' I said, and shook hands. Her seed eyes seemed underneath the earth. She held on to my hand. I felt as if I was held down in soil.

Ernest said, 'Goodbye, Miss Price,' and held out his hand, but hers still clutched mine. She beckoned to Mrs Rowan and whispered, 'The birds. I want to give her a bird,' and then to me, 'I want to give you a bird.'

Mrs Rowan walked into the next room and returned with a paper bag. Miss Price released my hand and dug down into the bag with shelving fingers. 'No, not these,' she said angrily. 'These are green.'

'They're the only ones,' Mrs Rowan said. 'The others have all gone.'

'I don't like them,' said Miss Price, holding one out on a beaded cord. It was stuffed green serge, dotted with red beadwork, and two red cherries hung from its mouth. 'It's paddy green,' she said disgustedly, and sucked in the corners of mouth.

'Never mind,' I said. 'It's lovely, and paddy green goes with my name. I'm Patricia, you see, and they sometimes call me Paddy.' I stood back in astonishment at my own sentences, and Miss Price gave an enormous shrug, which, for the moment until she released it, made her fill the room. And then, 'God!' she said, 'what a name!' The scorn in her voice shrivelled us. When I looked back at her as I left she had fallen into silent, shapeless laughter.

Mrs Rowan showed us downstairs and called the man servant to see us out. She stood like a child at the foot of the stairs and waved to us every few minutes as the grinning white-coated houseman helped us into our coats.

'You must come again and let Miss Price pour tea for you. It gives her such pleasure.'

Outside, on the step, I began to laugh. I had been impaled and had escaped. My laughter went on and on. It was loud, the people in the street stared at me.

Ernest looked at me with disapproval. 'What do you find so funny?' he asked.

What? What indeed? There was nothing funny at all. Nothing anywhere. But I poked about for an answer.

'Why, this,' I said, holding the bird by its beaded cord. 'This, of course.'

He looked at it a long time. 'Yes,' he said, seriously. 'Yes I suppose it is quaint,' and he smiled.

It was as though a pearl was smiling.

(1942)

The Neighbour

There was silence at the kitchen table, except for the noise of eating, when the bare leg came through the ceiling. Jeddy was stirring his tea loudly when it came down directly over the centre of the table, so covered with drops of water that it hung like a chandelier. A few splinters and drops fell onto the tablecloth and one or two dripped on the sliced tomatoes.

Mr Colley looked up from his hamburg steak, his long nose casting a wedge of shadow on his face as he tilted his head; the light caught his glasses giving the illusion of a face without eyes. 'Merrit!' he said and beat his two fists on the table so the plates jumped. 'What's he think, eh?' The leg waved about in the air, throwing water spots on the wallpaper.

'Leave off of soiling our walls, leave off.' Mrs Colley stood up and struck out at the foot with her fork. Her dress was short at the back. When she moved she showed her legs splaying out above the knees and extending into long purplish-blue bloomers. She struck at the bare wet foot and the leg lashed about like a snake.

'Jesus!' said Jeddy, watching the performance. He sat taut with pleasure. 'Hit him, Ma,' he said. His black hair was cut like a skull cap. He looked like a sadistic dwarf monk.

'Merrit, you leave us be,' said Mr Colley furiously. 'Always poking in our business. Leave us be,' he yelled to the leg, and the leg, as if in obedience, slowly shortened, went up through the ceiling and the water came down all over the table. It came like a great column, melting at its base and spreading out on the floor.

'First the walls and now the tea,' said Mrs Colley, pulling at the table and upsetting the pitcher of milk; pushing a rag into her husband's hands, jerkily sloshing the wet mop over the worn linoleum.

'What's he think, eh?' said Mr Colley on his knees and Merrit's voice came thick and adenoidish from the hole in the ceiling, 'Helpb muh, helpb. I'm in a jeezly bog.' You could see his face now when you looked up – the black holes of the nose and the lips hanging like dark fungus.

Mona shivered when she heard his voice and touched the frizzled ends of her hair with chipped scarlet fingernails. The thick wet rubber of his lips, the hands like bread poultices that waited in the hallway for her, waited under the well of the stairs in the darkness and caught her when she came in. She hated it and him, but she always stayed. And now she had seen his bare leg hanging in the light. Something heavy settled in her.

Jeddy ran for Mona's tartan umbrella, climbed on a chair, and, his face distorted with pleasure, poked at Merrit with its point. A low wheezing moan drained out of the mouth like a shaft of dust.

'Leave off of that.' Mr Colley pulled at Jeddy's sleeve. Jeddy doubled as if kicked in the stomach, his face stretched with laughter, his feet hitting the floor like pistons. 'Jesus, Jesus!' His laughter was high as a tin whistle in the room.

Mr Colley stood directly under the hole, hands on his hips and looked up. 'What d'ya think ya doin', eh? Ya nosey bastard. Always comin' where ya ain't deesirable.'

'I was ony havin' a bath – jes' takin' a bath,' said Merrit. 'Helpb muh, helpb. The tub flowed over and the floor's a jeezly bog. The whole ceiling'll fall, like enough,' he added ominously.

Mr and Mrs Colley both looked at the ceiling and then at the room, realizing together what it meant. Mrs Colley started pulling the furniture through the doorway. Mr Colley took command. 'Spread the weight out even, like you was on ice,' he called up. 'Then ease yourself gradual out into the hall.'

Mrs Colley stopped tugging at the table. 'He don't spread even,' she snapped. 'All of his weight's in his stomach.' And then she began tugging again. Mona shut her eyes and shook her head back and forth quickly. She felt sick.

'Yah! Yah! Ya can't skeer me no more now,' Jeddy screamed suddenly. 'Ya can't skeer me no more. Ya big sissy. If ya chase me agin I won't be skeered.' He grew large in the room as he spoke, like a pouter pigeon.

'I never did scare you none, Jeddy,' Merrit's voice wheedled. 'You jes' come up here, Jeddy, 'n helpb pull me outa this here jeezly bog, eh Jeddy?'

'I'll jeezly bog you,' said Jeddy hysterically and flung his body viciously about the room till he was dizzy. 'I'll jeezly bog you, ya bastard.'

The table was out in the hallway now and the chairs. Mrs Colley was looking at the stove. She laid her hands on it as if for the last time. 'That Merrit,' she said, but softly. 'That Merrit.'

'Now work yourself over easy,' Mr Colley was saying. Groans, bangs and bumps sounded from above. 'He's goin','' said Mr Colley. 'He's outa sight.' A few last drops of water fell. 'Now, Mona, you get and stuff that hole up with newspaper while your ma brings the table back.'

'I'm goin' out,' said Mona, her back turned.

'Oh, no, you ain't.' Mr Colley grabbed her shoulder. 'What d'ya think y'are, eh? Goin' out! You're goin' ta stay right here and do as I say.'

Mona lurched herself free. 'I'm goin' out, I tell ya. I'm goin' out.'

'You mind what yer dad tells yer.' Mrs Colley was bringing the table back again. 'D'ya think it's safe now?' She looked at the stove.

Mr Colley thrust his face up close to Mona's and spoke through still lips. 'You're goin' to stay right here and finish yer tea, see? That's what you're goin' ta do.' He pushed her onto a chair and she sat with a bump, opened her mouth wide and began to cry.

'Leave me be, leave me be. Ya never let me do anything. I'm goin' out, see. I'm goin' out.' But she made no movement, sat quite still in the chair, not even lifting her hands to cover her face.

'Yah! cry-baby, cry-baby.' Jeddy was alive again, dancing up and down before his sister. 'Cry-baby. Ya can't see your sweetheart. I seen ya in the hallway. I seen ya.'

Mr Colley was on a chair stuffing newspaper into the hole in the ceiling. He got down from the chair, found a pencil and paper and licking the lead began to write slowly. 'Listen to this,' he said, reading. 'Listen to this: Mind your own business from now on, see? When we want to see ya, we'll invite ya down special. Signed, William Colley.' He laughed so he had to loosen his belt and then climbed on the chair, pulled out the newspaper, stuck the note through and filled the hole again.

Jeddy was sitting at the wrecked table, hunched over his plate, shovelling the cold wet hamburger into his mouth.

'That'll fix Merrit,' said Mr Colley settling at his place. 'That'll fix him.' He picked up his fork and wiped it on his sleeve.

'Times like this I miss a phone somethin' awful,' Mrs Colley said. 'Would I ever like to ring up that Merrit and tell him what I think for spoiling our good tea.' Her face was drawn with the pleasure denied her. She took the plate of sliced tomatoes and rinsed them under the tap. 'I guess I don't feel much like eatin' now,' she said. 'That Merrit's leg kinda turned my stomach.' She sat down from habit and watched her husband and son.

There was silence again at the kitchen table, except for the noise of eating, Merrit lumbering overhead and Mona's chattering sobs.

(1942)

The Lord's Plan

Seamus carried his suitcase in his right hand. It was heavy and his feet were hot – swelling, bulging against the bumpy uppers of his shoes. His toes felt puffy and webbed.

The sun was in mid-heaven exactly. It shone on the top of his hat. The dent in his green fedora caught all the sun, held it in a pool. Seamus gave a dusty grin thinking of his suitcase, thinking of the Word of God – the Words of God – packed tightly layer upon layer.

His new sales psychology had worked.

The Lord had given him a plan to sell His Word. Only yesterday, while Seamus was lying in a haystack, airing his feet, the Lord had explained His Plan. He had heard the Lord say: 'Seamus, Lamb of the Lord, in order to sell my word you must have a plan.' Seamus had jolted forward in the hay. He had tried to convince himself that there was nothing strange in being spoken to by the Lord. But it *had* been strange, none the less.

Seamus had parked his gum behind his ear and stubbed his cigarette and put the butt in his breast pocket – the least he could do for the Lord. And then the Lord had boomed. His Voice had sounded like thunder and Seamus had looked up to the sky and found it blue and clear. The Lord had boomed, 'Psychology.' Seamus had nodded. It didn't do to let the Lord know he was an ignorant man. Seamus smiled and repeated the word 'psychology'. It rattled round in his head for a few minutes afterwards. But the Lord had been kind. He had explained the word, just as any Christian gentleman would do, pretending that Seamus knew it all the while.

And – but of course it would, as it was the Lord's Plan – it worked. At the very first house he had come to, it had worked. He had stopped at the door of a farmhouse and knocked. A woman opened it. She was pale and immense as though she were made of bread dough, Seamus thought, and had been rising before the kitchen range for years – rising and swelling. Seamus looked at her arms hanging from her sleeveless dress. She had said, 'What would you want?' And he had almost forgotten to answer her, almost forgotten the Lord's Plan, because after her arms he had seen her stomach and then he had had to remind himself that he was on the Lord's business. By that time she had noticed his bag and she had said, 'Salesman?' How her eyes had folded under the fat lids – how the brown slits that showed through had looked like molasses in the sun; and how close Seamus had come to walking away, then and there, quickly.

But he remembered the Lord's Plan.

He put down his bag and said, 'I'm tired, I've walked a long way. Could I –' and he smiled, 'come in and rest a minute?'

The bulk in the doorway had moved. Seamus stepped inside the large kitchen and sat down. He put his suitcase on the kitchen table. She looked at it once or twice. He pretended it wasn't there. He passed the time of day with her as she beat cookie batter. He watched the flesh of her arms flowing free from the bone, flapping, flapping, flapping; and then her stomach, like a large jelly, wobbling, shivering, under the flowered dress. When she moved one part of her, all moved.

He said, 'Could I fetch a cup of water from the well? There is dust in my mouth.' She lowered the dipper into a water bucket and handed it to him, dripping. He could see the drops of water on the dipper's lip sparkling. It was all part of the Lord's Plan. He drank. He hung the dipper on the nail again. He thought of that himself. It was as the Lord would have done. He went back to his seat. She kept turning to look at his suitcase. And then he said, 'D'you mind if I smoke?' She shook her head. He waited a minute until her flesh had quietened. That one shake had started her arms, her belly, her buttocks. He stopped in horror at the words in his mind and he opened his suitcase for his makings. For now, now, the psychology would really begin. As he lifted the lid he saw the booklets piled neatly – booklets of the Lord. But he pretended he didn't notice them and he took out his tobacco and rolled a cigarette. She came over to the suitcase, chose a spoon from a drawer in the table and looked at the booklets in the bag. She returned to the batter, dipped it out into little hummocks on a pan. But in a minute she came back. She put out a finger like a large pale sausage with a little bit of gristle shining at the end of it. She touched one of the booklets and left a smudge of cookie dough on it. 'Books,' she said.

He feigned unconcern. 'Yes, books.' He waited, examining the end of his cigarette.

She turned the pages. 'Words, words,' she said.

'Yes, God's.'

'Oh, God's?'

'Yes.' He blew smoke out through his nose. 'Take a look,' he said.

It had all been so easy. But then it had been the Lord's Plan. She bought.

He finished his cigarette, fastened his suitcase and walked to the door, but on the way – ah, if only the Lord had helped him there! – as he passed her, his hand shot out and fell on her buttocks, hard enough to start her flesh jiggling again. And he had laughed. She picked up the spoon and brought it down on his head. It had hurt. She used words too – words he wanted to forget, being on the Lord's Business. He had decided she was a very common woman.

He laughed now when he thought of it, even though the sun was hot and the lump on his head ached where his hat pressed on it. If he'd done that to a pretty girl she'd have liked it; and anyway that was *his* psychology – make up to the ladies. True, the Lord hadn't suggested it, but it had always worked before, so he might as well keep on. And too, the next house he had come to after that, hadn't it worked? It sure had. But it was a girl there, young and pretty. Her eyes had flashed when he had chucked her under the chin and she'd tossed her head and said, 'You're some smart, you are.' Some smart! He'd say he was. Seamus O'Reilly, never seen Ireland, Salesman in the Lord's Business. Some smart! And she was some smart too – some pretty. He thought of her as he walked. He forgot his feet.

At the end of the blueberry plains there was a store. Gasoline pumps outside and signs on the store. He thought of the Lord's Plan. He thought of the sun in a pool in the dent of his hat. He walked into the store. It was dark and he couldn't see much at first. A girl's voice inquired, 'Selling?'

'Nothing that'd interest you,' he said. He ordered a bottle of lime rickey and it walked across the counter to him. Imagine that! He was going to say something to the girl about it but she interrupted him.

'How d'you know?' she asked.

He laid his suitcase beside him and tapped it saying, 'Because it's not candy or cosmetics or silk stockings' – but not before he'd noticed the girl. Not too bad, but drab. He figured his plan and the Lord's together ought to make this sale a cinch. He drank up the lime rickey and ordered another bottle. Boy, how those bottles could walk!

'How's business?' he asked.

'Not bad,' she answered. 'How's yours?'

'Good,' he said. 'Better and better. See a pretty face and business is swell.' He watched her as he said it. She smirked and poked a pound of bacon on the counter. And he forgot the Lord's Plan. She walked round beside him. He put his arm round her waist and squeezed her. She pulled away a little.

'Fresh, eh?'

He laughed.

'What you sellin'?'

He saw her eye his suitcase. 'Wouldn't you like to know!'

'Come on, give!'

'Maybe I don't sell. Maybe I'm a college guy hitch-hikin' to college.'

'Maybe I'm a pair of chickens!'

'Maybe you are.' He squeezed her again. She wriggled and looked down. Stuck out her tongue a little. It was pink like a kitten's.

'What's your name?'

'Mabel. What's yours?'

'Seamus.'

'Gee! what a handle.'

It was the way she said 'handle' that did it. The way her mouth opened and her lips curled. It wasn't his fault. He kissed her. She was like barbed wire in his arms then. The way she pulled away, bristling, spiked with anger. She hauled back her hand and slapped his face. Women! He loved them. He caught her hand, kissed the palm of it, laughing. She walked away. But her hand ... he still held it. Saints alive! It had come off. She looked black. She stumped away into the darkness, her arm hanging, handless.

He looked at the hand. The skin was rough, red a little, and the nails were like small pearl buttons sewn on the fingers. He was alone in the store with the hand; the hand wearing a gold ring with 'M' on it. He slipped the ring off; he had no right to that; it was hers.

And then he remembered the Lord's Plan. And he knew. The Lord was reminding him to use His Psychology. This was the Lord's Way – miracles.

He opened his suitcase and saw the Lord's Word. He took out a booklet and laid it on the counter, with the ring on top of it. He thought of that himself. It was as the Lord would have done. And he packed the hand in the suitcase. That would remind him of the Lord's Plan, remind him to keep about the Lord's Business. The Lord was looking after His Own. Seamus understood.

He snapped the fasteners on his bag and put on his hat and walked out into the sunshine. He gave a happy grin thinking of his suitcase – thinking of the Word of God – the Words of God – packed tightly layer on layer; thinking of the hand, God's Miracle, God's Reminder.

He pushed his hat back so it didn't press on the bump on his head. He took an old stub from his breast pocket and lit up. Gee! He gave a long whistle of pleasure. Seamus O'Reilly, never seen Ireland, Salesman in the Lord's Business, some smart.

He'd say!

(1942)

Miracles

That evening after supper while Madame rocked on the gallery in the slowly settling darkness Annette took us to see her friends. Lights blazed in the windows as we walked with dust muffled steps along the village street and the air was flooded with green as though chlorophyll lit the evening.

Small groups of youths walked by, serious and stolid as moose in their pin striped suits. *'Salut'*, *'Bon soir'* – the greetings rang out as they passed. Annette was proud in her acknowledgements, walking with a strange stiff-legged self-consciousness. Watching them I was amazed that there were no girls with them – no girls with their heavily powdered faces, extraordinary amateur curls and the stifling smell of cheap perfume.

'They have no girls?' I asked.

Annette was quick to assure me they had.

'But on an evening like this?'

'They are on their way to call,' Annette said.

'But they don't go out together?'

Annette swung horrified eyes to God at the suggestion. The *curé* did not allow it. The curé knew what was right for them and what was wrong. The curé knew everything and looked after them. The curé said it was wicked.

Luke walked, his hands in his pockets, his head back, saying nothing. At first I dragged him into the conversation but when Annette began to talk of the curé I forgot. Besides, I

A section from an unfinished novel, *The Lion in the Streets*.

needed all my energy to keep up with her, to follow the acrobatics of her speech.

'He is a very great and good man,' said Annette and her words sounded staccato on the long quiet street. 'He performs miracles.' The speed and extravagance of Annette's language made me feel that I was in some way inside a catherine wheel.

Her face grew long and full of wonder as she recounted her miracle. 'Until I was twenty-one,' she said, 'I was not like other girls. I had been unwell and I was very weak. Mamma was worried about me. All my sisters were strong, they were getting married, but I was not and each month we waited and I was not well. Mamma got the horse and cart from the Pagets' and we drove to the town. It was a long way. And it is very expensive to see the doctor. Mamma had the money in her hand and I was afraid when we arrived. It was hot and my head was full and I was ashamed. We waited for him to come and then we told him. He took the money Mamma had in her hand and gave me some medicine and we drove back home again. All that way, all that money, all that way home again. I took the medicine he gave and waited. Each month I waited. Each morning I went to early Mass and prayed but nothing happened. And all the time I got sicker and sicker. Mamma went to the curé then and he came. He said he would perform a miracle. He got a big glass and a bottle of porter and he poured the porter into the glass. Then he added two teaspoons of mustard and he stirred and stirred until it was frothing. He handed me the glass. "Drink it down while it is still frothing," he said. But I couldn't. I shook my head. I could not drink that drink. "Drink it down while it is frothing and you will be cured within five minutes." I saw the big glass. Mamma was crying. "Drink it down," said Mamma and she held her head in her hands and rocked from side to side. 'Drink it down, Annette.' Then I didn't care any more. I took the big glass and I thought of the face of the Virgin Mary and I made the sign of the Cross and prayed inside me and I drank it down. It was bad, that drink. It tasted bad. I wanted to be sick to my stomach.' Annette paused and gave a great sigh as if she had lived the whole experience over again.

'And it worked?' I asked.

The story finished, Annette nodded her head sagely, smugly 'Ah, yes. It was a miracle. A miracle in the name of God.'

'And you've been all right ever since?' the tale shocked me. In my own head I saw a black-robed curé – Mamma, great fat Mamma, shaking her head and crying and Annette drinking down a devil's brew with its smoking sulphur-coloured fumes that changed her from a child into a woman in five minutes 'Ever since you have been all right?'

'Ah, but yes, it was a miracle.'

Had the curé performed other miracles? I wanted to know. What else had he done?

Annette pursed her lips and shrugged. 'Ah, yes.'

'Tell me,' I said, but we had already arrived at the Simone's. Another time she would tell me. Now her mind was on her friends. They were especially beautiful, Annette informed us, for they were blond. And that was rare. They were the only people in the village who were blond.

On the gallery sat Mme Simone, frail as a Marie Laurençin painting, her high cheekbones dotted with excited crimson, her hair permanented like the fizz on ginger beer. She rocked more slowly as she greeted Annette and was introduced, insisted that we all sit down, brought forward chairs, smiled nervously and moved her white hands across her apron. Noiselessly, as wherever we went, the children collected – stood in silence, pale, alarmingly pale; each with the dot of tubercular rouge on their cheekbones, their uncurled hair smooth on their heads as butter, their legs and arms motionless.

The ground sloped up from the house beside us – grass and apple trees with yellow apples luminous in the leaves, lying in the grass pale as the children's hair – and everything tinged with the green light, washed in it.

While Mme Simone and Annette gossiped I felt bathed in the blond and green incandescence of this family and its garden, and was fascinated and appalled by the still life of the children, the shyness that held them fixed and their flax-blue eyes that looked as shallow and delicate as petals.

'André has bought a truck,' Annette said and her pride sat upon her fat and sleek as mercury, before it broke and scattered in excited description. 'It is big,' she said, her arms enclosing it. 'The whole village could ride in it, it is so big. And it is red.'

'Agathe told me,' said Mme Simone. Her eyelids lifted to hoods and she pursed her mouth to judgement. 'He gets a truck instead of a wife,' she said. 'It is not good.'

'It makes a beautiful noise,' said Annette, like a child. She turned to us. 'It makes a better noise than your car.'

'Where is it?' I asked. 'Why haven't we seen it?'

'André has gone to the city already.'

Madame nodded sagely. 'Soon André will live in the city,' she announced.

Luke knocked the ashes from his pipe, blew through it a couple of times and put it in his pocket.

The greenness grew deeper as we talked – came up and swamped us until it seemed as if we were under the sea. Mme Simone became nervous, rocked rapidly, and suddenly her harsh voice commanded the children: 'Get apples for the English.' But the children hardly moved. A slight tremor of increased shyness rippled them and froze them. Raising her voice to an alarming volume the mother repeated her command and they scuttled then, uncannily green, into the deep grass, picking the globes of fruit from the ground, reaching to the lower branches of the trees, moving with their eyes still on Luke and me; shy, offering their harvest with white-green fingers, smiles making masks of their small faces.

I held out my hand to receive the clusters of fruit with the leaves attached.

'They are flower apples,' the mother said, and Annette, nibbling, explained that they didn't last, but faded like flowers in a few days.

The giant illuminated cross on the hillside sharpened and brightened as the darkness fell. Proudly they nodded at it, Annette and Mme Simone, drew down the corners of their mouths, told how it burned day and night, day and night, and how it was their cross, how each family paid for a light and that light never went out.

In Annette's charge, we left when she gave the sign. The green light was deeper now, the children behind their mother seemed no longer strange, but terrible – tiny and fair and lifeless while Madame rocked unceasingly back and forth in her chair, and beside them, on the hillside, the vegetation crept in closer and closer like a wave.

Leaving, our apples still in our hands, Annette said, 'Eat them. They are good.' But I shook my head, feeling the perfectly formed and infected fruit against my palms – pale apple-green and deadly.

'Are they not beautiful, the Simones?' Annette was anxious to know. 'Are they not the most beautiful people you have seen here?'

'But surely,' I said, sick with alarm, 'Surely they are ill. Consumptive?'

'Ah yes,' said Annette in easy agreement, but bored.

'But Annette, it is a dangerous disease. It is catching. It will spread.'

'No!' Annette's voice was incredulous. 'You joke,' she said and laughed.

I felt desperate. I wanted to convince Annette. 'In the city,' I said, 'those people would go away for treatment. Doesn't the doctor see them, Annette?'

Annette was not interested. 'It is nothing,' she said. 'The Bouchards have it and the Pagets and the ...' she listed the family names. 'It is nothing. The curé goes and he prays. Sometimes it gets bad and someone dies. Often that happens.'

I wanted to cry out at Annette's stupidity. I grabbed Luke's arm. 'Say something to her,' I said. 'Tell her, Luke.'

'It is a dangerous illness,' Luke said. And the subject was finished. But something violent and terrible was happening inside me. An anger I had not known before, a fury at the ignorance and pitifulness of people. I had hoped for some affirmation of a similar feeling in Luke. But his voice had been factual and indifferent. I let go his arm quickly, and when he felt for my hand in the darkness and tried to hold it I pulled away, even knowing that he too, needed affirming at that moment.

We stumbled a little in the darkness on the dusty road. A smell of salt blew up from the river and the houses were quiet as though deserted. It was as if all the inhabitants were dead – and the faces of the Simone children arranged themselves before my eyes, lying like wax and butter in a row of green wood coffins.

The curé goes and he prays. The curé is a great and good man. The curé performs miracles. But there are no miracles in the consumptive houses, I thought. No miracles there and I was bitter with Annette for her dreadful acceptance of death. Bitter with Annette and furious with Luke.

(1944)

Unless the Eye Catch Fire

> Unless the eye catch fire
> The God will not be seen ...
> *Where the Wasteland Ends*, Theodore Rosak

Wednesday, September 17. The day began normally enough. The quail cockaded as antique foot soldiers, arrived while I was having my breakfast. The males black-faced, white-necklaced, cinnamon-crowned, with short, sharp, dark plumes. Square bibs, Payne's grey; belly and sides with a pattern of small stitches. Reassuring, the flock of them. They tell me the macadamization of the world is not complete.

A sudden alarm, and as if they had one brain among them, they were gone in a rush – a sideways ascending Niagara – shutting out the light, obscuring the sky and exposing a rectangle of lawn, unexpectedly emerald. How bright the berries on the cotoneaster. Random leaves on the cherry twirled like gold spinners. The garden was high-keyed, vivid, locked in aspic.

Without warning, and as if I were looking down the tube of a kaleidoscope, the merest shake occurred – moiréed the garden – rectified itself. Or, more precisely, as if a range-finder through which I had been sighting found of itself a more accurate focus. Sharpened, in fact, to an excoriating exactness.

And then the colours changed. Shifted to a higher octave – a *bright spectrum*. Each colour with its own *light*, its own *shape*. The leaves of the trees, the berries, the grasses – as if shedding successive films – disclosed layer after layer of hidden perfections. And upon these rapidly changing surfaces the 'range-finder' – to really play hob with metaphor! – sharpened its small invisible blades.

I don't know how to describe the intensity and speed of focus of this gratuitous zoom lens through which I stared, or the swift and dizzying adjustments within me. I became a 'sleeping top,' perfectly centred, perfectly sighted. The colours vibrated beyond the visible range of the spectrum. Yet I saw them. With some matching eye. Whole galaxies of them, blazing and glowing, flowing in rivulets, gushing in fountains – volatile, mercurial, and making lacklustre and off-key the colours of the rainbow.

I had no time or inclination to wonder, intellectualize. My mind seemed astonishingly clear and quite still. Like a crystal. A burning glass.

And then the range-finder sharpened once again. To alter space.

The lawn, the bushes, the trees – still super-brilliant – were no longer *there*. *There*, in fact, had ceased to exist. They were now, of all places in the world, *here*. Right in the centre of my being. Occupying an immense inner space. Part of me. Mine. Except the whole idea of ownership was beside the point. As true to say I was theirs as they mine. I and they were here; they and I, there. (*There, here* ... odd ... but for an irrelevant, inconsequential 't' which comes and goes, the words are the same.)

As suddenly as the world had altered, it returned to normal. I looked at my watch. A ridiculous mechanical habit. As I had no idea when the experience began it was impossible to know how long it had lasted. What had seemed eternity couldn't have been more than a minute or so. My coffee was still steaming in its mug.

The garden, through the window, was as it had always been. Yet not as it had always been. Less. Like listening to mono after hearing stereo. But with a far greater loss of dimension. A grievous loss.

I rubbed my eyes. Wondered, not without alarm, if this was

160

the onset of some disease of the retina – glaucoma or some cellular change in the eye itself – superlatively packaged, fatally sweet as the marzipan cherry I ate as a child and *knew* was poison. If it *is* a disease, the symptoms will recur. It will happen again.

Tuesday, September 23. It *has* happened again.

Tonight, taking Dexter for his late walk, I looked up at the crocheted tangle of boughs against the sky. Dark silhouettes against the lesser dark, but beating now with an extraordinary black brilliance. The golden glints in obsidian or the lurking embers in black opals are the nearest I can come to describing them. But it's a false description, emphasizing as it does the wrong end of the scale. This was a *dark spectrum.* As if the starry heavens were translated into densities of black – black Mars, black Saturn, black Jupiter; or a master jeweller had crossed his jewels with jet and set them to burn and wink in the branches and twigs of oaks whose leaves shone luminous – a leafy Milky Way – fired by black chlorophyll.

Dexter stopped as dead as I. Transfixed. His thick honey-coloured coat and amber eyes, glowing with their own intense brightness, suggested yet another spectrum. A *spectrum of light.* He was a constellated dog, shining, supra-real, against the foothills and mountain ranges of midnight.

I am reminded now, as I write, of a collection of lepidoptera in Brazil – one entire wall covered with butterflies, creatures of daylight – enormous or tiny – blue, orange, black. Strong-coloured. And on the opposite wall their antiselves – pale night flyers spanning such a range of silver and white and lightest snuff-colour that once one entered their spectral scale there was no end to the subleties and delicate nuances. But I didn't think like this then. All thought, all comparisons were prevented by the startling infinities of darkness and light.

Then, as before, the additional shake occurred and the two spectrums moved swiftly from without to within. As if two equal and complementary circles centred inside me – or I in them. How explain that I not only *saw* but actually *was* the two spectrums? (I underline a simple, but in this case exactly appropriate, anagram.)

Then the range-finder lost its focus and the world, once again, was back to normal. Dexter, a pale, blurred blob, bounded about within the field of my peripheral vision, going on with his doggy interests just as if a moment before he had not been frozen in his tracks, a dog entranced.

I am no longer concerned about my eyesight. Wonder only if we are both mad, Dexter and I? Angelically mad, sharing hallucinations of epiphany. *Folie à deux?*

Friday, October 3. It's hard to account for my secrecy, for I *have* been secretive. As if the cat had my tongue. It's not that I don't long to talk about the colours but I can't risk the wrong response – (as Gaby once said of a companion after a faultless performance of *Giselle:* 'If she had criticized the least detail of it, I'd have hit her!').

Once or twice I've gone so far as to say, 'I had the most extraordinary experience the other day ...' hoping to find some look or phrase, some answering, 'So did I.' None has been forthcoming.

I can't forget the beauty. Can't get it out of my head. Startling, unearthly, indescribable. Infuriatingly indescribable. A glimpse of – somewhere else. Somewhere alive, miraculous, newly made yet timeless. And more important still – significant, luminous, with a meaning of which I was part. Except that I – the I who is writing this – did not exist: was flooded out, dissolved in that immensity where subject and object are one.

I have to make a deliberate effort now not to live my life in terms of it; not to sit, immobilized, awaiting the shake that heralds a new world. Awaiting the transfiguration.

Luckily the necessities of life keep me busy. But upstream of my actions, behind a kind of plate glass, some part of me waits, listens, maintains a total attention.

Tuesday, October 7. Things are moving very fast.

Some nights ago my eye was caught by a news item. 'Trucker Blames Colours,' went the headline. Reading on: 'R.T. Ballantyne, driver for Island Trucks, failed to stop on a red light at the intersection of Fernhill and Spender. Questioned by traffic police, Ballantyne replied: "I didn't see it, that's all. There was this shake, then all these colours suddenly in the trees. Real bright ones I'd never seen before. I guess they must have blinded me." A breathalyzer test proved negative.' Full stop.

I had an overpowering desire to talk to R.T. Ballantyne. Even looked him up in the telephone book. Not listed. I debated reaching him through Island Trucks in the morning.

Hoping for some mention of the story, I switched on the local radio station, caught the announcer mid-sentence:

'... to come to the studio and talk to us. So far no one has been able to describe just what the "new" colours are, but perhaps Ruby Howard can. Ruby, you say you actually *saw* "new" colours?'

What might have been a flat, rather ordinary female voice was sharpened by wonder. 'I was out in the garden, putting it to bed, you might say, getting it ready for winter. The hydrangeas are dried out – you know the way they go. Soft beiges and greys. And I was thinking maybe I should cut them back, when there was this – shake, like – and there they were shining. Pink. And blue. But not like they are in life. Different. Brighter. With little lights, like ...'

The announcer's voice cut in, 'You say "not like they are in life". D'you think this wasn't life? I mean, do you think maybe you were dreaming?'

'Oh, no,' answered my good Mrs Howard, positive, clear, totally unrattled. 'Oh, no, I wasn't *dreaming*. Not *dreaming* – ... Why – *this* is more like dreaming.' She was quiet a moment and then, in a matter-of-fact voice, 'I can't expect you to believe it,' she said. 'Why should you? I wouldn't believe it myself if I hadn't seen it.' Her voice expressed a kind of compassion as if she was really sorry for the announcer.

I picked up the telephone book for the second time, looked up the number of the station. I had decided to tell Mrs Howard what I had seen. I dialled, got a busy signal, depressed the bar and waited, cradle in hand. I dialled again. And again.

Later. J. just phoned. Curious how she and I play the same game over and over.

J: Were you watching Channel 8?

ME: No, I ...

J: An interview. With a lunatic. One who sees colours and flashing lights.

ME: Tell me about it.

J: He was a logger – a high-rigger – not that that has anything to do with it. He's retired now and lives in an apartment and has a window-box with geraniums. This morning the flowers were like neon, he said, flashing and shining ... *Honestly!*

ME: Perhaps he saw something you can't ...

J: (*Amused*) I might have known you'd take his side. Seriously, what *could* he have seen?

ME: Flashing and shining – as he said.

J: But they couldn't. Not geraniums. And you know it as well as I do. *Honestly*, Babe ... (She is the only person left who calls me the name my mother called me.) Why are you always so perverse?

I felt faithless. I put down the receiver, as if I had not borne witness to my God.

October 22. Floods of letters to the papers. Endless interviews on radio and TV. Pros, cons, inevitable spoofs.

One develops an eye for authenticity. It's as easy to spot as sunlight. However they may vary in detail, true accounts of the colours have an unmistakable common factor – a common factor as difficult to convey as sweetness to those who know only salt. True accounts are inarticulate, diffuse, unlikely – impossible.

It's recently crossed my mind that there may be some relationship between having seen the colours and their actual manifestation – something as improbable as *the more one sees them the more they are able to be seen.* Perhaps they are always there in some normally invisible part of the electro-magnetic spectrum and only become visible to certain people at certain times. A combination of circumstances or some subtle refinement in the organ of sight. And then – from quantity to quality perhaps, like water to ice – a whole community changes, is able to see, catches fire.

For example, it was seven days between the first time I saw the colours and the second. During that time there were no reports to the media. But once the reports began, the time between lessened appreciably *for me.* Not proof, of course, but worth noting. And I can't help wondering why some people see the colours and others don't. Do some of us have extra vision? Are some so conditioned that they're virtually blind to what's there before their very noses? Is it a question of more, or less?

Reports come in from farther and farther afield; from all walks of life. I think now there is no portion of the inhabited globe without 'shake freaks' and no acceptable reason for the sightings. Often, only one member of a family will testify to the heightened vision. In my own small circle, I am the only witness – or so I think. I feel curiously hypocritical as I listen to my friends denouncing the 'shakers'. Drugs, they say. Irrational – possibly dangerous. Although no sinister incidents have

165

occurred yet – just some mild shake-baiting here and there –
one is uneasily reminded of Salem.

Scientists pronounce us hallucinated or mistaken, pointing
out that so far there is no hard evidence, no objective proof.
That means, I suppose, no photographs, no spectroscopic mea-
surement – if such is possible. Interestingly, seismographs show
very minor earthquake tremors – showers of them, like shooting stars in August. Pundits claim 'shake fever' – as it has come
to be called – is a variant on flying saucer fever and that it will
subside in its own time. Beneficent physiologists suggest we are
suffering (why is it *always* suffering, never enjoying?) a distorted form of *ocular spectrum* or after-image. (An after-image
of what?) Psychologists disagree among themselves. All in all,
it is not surprising that some of us prefer to keep our experi-
ences to ourselves.

January 9. Something new has occurred. Something impossible. Disturbing. So disturbing, in fact, that according to
rumour it is already being taken with the utmost seriousness at
the highest levels. TV, press and radio – with good reason – talk
of little else.

What seemingly began as a mild winter has assumed sinister
overtones. Farmers in southern Alberta are claiming the earth
is unnaturally hot to the touch. Golfers at Harrison complain
that the soles of their feet burn. Here on the coast, we notice it
less. Benign winters are our specialty.

Already we don't lack for explanations as to why the earth
could not be hotter than usual, nor why it is naturally 'un-nat-
urally' hot. Vague notes of reassurance creep into the speeches
of public men. They may be unable to explain the issue, but
they can no longer ignore it.

To confuse matters further, reports on temperatures seem
curiously inconsistent. What information we get comes mainly
from self-appointed 'earth touchers'. And now that the least

thing can fire an argument, their conflicting readings lead often enough to inflammatory debate.

For myself, I can detect no change at all in my own garden.

Thursday...? There is no longer any doubt. The temperature of the earth's surface *is* increasing.

It is unnerving, horrible, to go out and feel the ground like some great beast, warm, beneath one's feet. As if another presence – vast, invisible – attends one. Dexter, too, is perplexed. He barks at the earth with the same indignation and, I suppose, fear, with which he barks at the first rumblings of earthquake.

Air temperatures, curiously, don't increase proportionately – or so we're told. It doesn't make sense, but at the moment nothing makes sense. Countless explanations have been offered. Elaborate explanations. None adequate. The fact that the air temperature remains temperate despite the higher ground heat must, I think, be helping to keep panic down. Even so, these are times of great tension.

Hard to understand these two unexplained – unrelated? – phenomena: the first capable of dividing families; the second menacing us all. We are like animals trapped in a burning building.

Later. J. just phoned. Terrified. Why don't I move in with her, she urges. After all she has the space and we have known each other forty years. (Hard to believe when I don't feel even forty!) She can't bear it – the loneliness.

Poor J. Always so protected, insulated by her money. And her charm. What one didn't provide, the other did ... diversions, services, attention.

What do I think is responsible for the heat, she asks. But it turns out she means who. Her personal theory is that the 'shake-freaks' are causing it – involuntarily, perhaps, but the two are surely linked.

'How could they possibly cause it?' I enquire. 'By what reach of the imagination ...?'

'Search *me!*' she protests. 'How on earth should *I* know?' And the sound of the dated slang makes me really laugh.

But suddenly she is close to tears. 'How can you *laugh?*' she calls. 'This is nightmare. Nightmare!'

Dear J. I wish I could help but the only comfort I could offer would terrify her still more.

September. Summer calmed us down. If the earth was hot, well, summers *are* hot. And we were simply having an abnormally hot one.

Now that it is fall – the season of cool nights, light frosts – and the earth like a feverish child remains worryingly hot, won't cool down, apprehension mounts.

At last we are given official readings. For months the authorities have assured us with irrefutable logic that the temperature of the earth could not be increasing. Now, without any apparent period of indecision or confusion, they are warning us with equal conviction and accurate statistical documentation that it has, in fact, increased. Something anyone with a pocket-handkerchief of lawn has known for some time.

Weather stations, science faculties, astronomical observatories all over the world are measuring and reporting. Intricate computerized tables are quoted. Special departments of Government have been set up. We speak now of a new Triassic Age – the Neo-Triassic – and of the accelerated melting of the ice caps. But we are elaborately assured that this could not, repeat not, occur in our lifetime.

Interpreters and analysts flourish. The media are filled with theories and explanations. The increased temperature has been attributed to impersonal agencies such as bacteria from outer space; a thinning of the earth's atmosphere; a build-up of carbon-dioxide in the air; some axial irregularity; a change in the earth's core (geologists are reported to have begun test borings). No theory is too far-fetched to have its supporters. And because man likes a scapegoat, blame has been laid upon NASA, atomic physicists, politicians, the occupants of flying saucers and finally upon mankind at large – improvident, greedy mankind – whose polluted, strike-ridden world is endangered now by the fabled flames of hell.

Yet, astonishingly, life goes on. The Pollack baby was born last week. I received the news as if it were a death. Nothing has brought the irony of our situation home to me so poignantly. And when I saw the perfect little creature in its mother's arms, the look of adoration on her face, I found myself saying the things one always says to a new mother – exactly as if the world had not changed. Exactly as if our radio was not informing us that Nostradamus, the Bible, and Jeane Dixon have all foreseen our plight. A new paperback, *Let Edgar Cayce Tell You Why* sold out in a matter of days. Attendance at churches has doubled. Cults proliferate. Yet even in this atmosphere, we, the 'shake freaks', are considered lunatic fringe. Odd men out. In certain quarters I believe we are seriously held responsible for the escalating heat, so J. is not alone. There have now been one or two nasty incidents. It is not surprising that even the most vocal among us have grown less willing to talk. I am glad to have kept silent. As a woman living alone, the less I draw attention to myself the better.

But, at the same time, we have suddenly all become neighbours. Total strangers greet each other on the street. And the almost invisible couple behind the high hedge appears every time I pass with Dexter – wanting to talk. Desperately wanting to talk.

For our lives are greatly altered by this overhanging sense of doom. It is already hard to buy certain commodities. Dairy products are in very short supply. On the other hand, the market is flooded with citrus fruits. We are threatened with severe shortages for the future. The authorities are resisting rationing but it will have to come, if only to prevent artificial shortages resulting from hoarding.

Luckily the colours are an almost daily event. I see them now, as it were, with my entire being. It is as if all my cells respond to their brilliance and become light too. At such times I feel I might shine in the dark.

No idea of the date. It is evening and I am tired but I am so far behind in my notes I want to get something down. Events have moved too fast for me.

Gardens, parks – every tillable inch of soil – have been appropriated for food crops. As an able, if aging body, with an acre of land and some knowledge of gardening, I have been made responsible for soybeans – small trifoliate plants rich with the promise of protein. Neat rows of them cover what were once my vegetable garden, flower beds, lawn.

Young men from the Department of Agriculture came last month, bulldozed, cultivated, planted. Efficient, noisy desecrators of my twenty years of landscaping. Dexter barked at them from the moment they appeared and I admit I would have shared his indignation had the water shortage not already created its own desolation.

As a Government gardener I'm a member of a new privileged class. I have watering and driving permits and coupons for gasoline and boots – an indication of what is to come. So far there has been no clothes rationing.

Daily instructions – when to water and how much, details of mulching, spraying – reach me from the Government radio station to which I tune first thing in the morning. It also provides temperature readings, weather forecasts and the latest news releases on emergency measures, curfews, rationing, insulation. From the way things are going I think it will soon be our only station. I doubt that newspapers will be able to print much longer. In any event, I have already given them up. At first it was interesting to see how quickly drugs, pollution, education, women's lib., all became bygone issues; and, initially, I was fascinated to see how we rationalized. Then I became bored. Then disheartened. Now I am too busy.

Evening. A call came from J. Will I come for Christmas?

Christmas! Extraordinary thought. Like a word from another language learned in my youth, now forgotten.

'I've still got some Heidseck. We can get tight.'

The word takes me back to my teens. 'Like old times ...'

'Yes.' She is eager. I hate to let her down. 'J., I can't. How could I get to you?'

'In your *car*, silly. *You* still have gas. You're the only one of us who has.' Do I detect a slight hint of accusation, as if I had acquired it illegally?

'But J., it's only for emergencies.'

'My God, Babe, d'you think *this* isn't an emergency?'

'J., dear ...'

'*Please*, Babe,' she pleads. 'I'm so afraid. Of the looters. The eeriness. You must be afraid too. *Please!*'

I should have said, yes, that of course I was afraid. It's only natural to be afraid. Or, unable to say that, I should have made the soothing noises a mother makes to her child. Instead, 'There's no reason to be afraid, J.,' I said. It must have sounded insufferably pompous.

'No reason!' She was exasperated with me. 'I'd have thought there was every reason.'

She will phone again. In the night perhaps when she can't sleep. Poor J. She feels so alone. She *is* so alone. And so idle. I don't suppose it's occurred to her yet that telephones will soon go. That a whole way of life is vanishing completely.

It's different for me. I have the soybeans which keep me busy all the daylight hours. And Dexter. And above all I have the colours and with them the knowledge that there are others, other people, whose sensibilities I share. We are as invisibly, inviolably related to one another as the components of a molecule. I say 'we'. Perhaps I should speak only for myself, yet I feel as sure of these others as if they had spoken. Like the quail, we share one brain – no, I think it is one heart – between us. How do I know this? How *do* I know? I know by knowing. We are less alarmed by the increasing heat than those who have not seen the colours. I can't explain why. But seeing the colours seems to change one – just as certain diagnostic procedures cure the complaint they are attempting to diagnose.

In all honesty I admit to having had moments when this sense of community was not enough, when I have had a great longing for my own kind – for so have I come to think of these others – in the way one has a great longing for someone one loves. Their presence in the world is not enough. One must see them. Touch them. Speak with them.

But lately that longing has lessened. All longing, in fact. And fear. Even my once great dread that I might cease to see the colours has vanished. It is as if through seeing them I have learned to see them. Have learned to be ready to see – passive; not striving to see – active. It keeps me very wide awake. Transparent even. Still.

The colours come daily now. Dizzying. Transforming. Lifegiving. My sometimes back-breaking toil in the garden is lightened, made full of wonder, by the incredible colours shooting in the manner of children's sparklers from the plants themselves and from my own work-worn hands. I hadn't realized that I too am part of this vibrating luminescence.

Later. I have no idea how long it is since I abandoned these notes. Without seasons to measure its passing, without normal activities – preparations for festivals, occasional outings – time feels longer, shorter or – more curious still – simultaneous, undifferentiated. Future and past fused in the present. Linearity broken.

I had intended to write regularly, but the soybeans keep me busy pretty well all day and by evening I'm usually ready for bed. I'm sorry however to have missed recording the day-by-day changes. They were more or less minor at first. But once the heat began its deadly escalation, the world as we have known it – 'our world' – had you been able to put it alongside 'this world' – would have seemed almost entirely different.

No one, I think, could have foreseen the speed with which everything has broken down. For instance, the elaborate plans made to maintain transportation became useless in a matter of months. Private traffic was first curtailed, then forbidden. If a man from another planet had looked in on us, he would have been astonished to see us trapped who were apparently free.

The big changes only really began after the first panic evacuations from the cities. Insulated by concrete, sewer pipes and underground parkades, high density areas responded slowly to the increasing temperatures. But once the heat penetrated their insulations, Gehennas were created overnight and whole populations fled in hysterical exodus, jamming highways in their futile attempts to escape.

Prior to this the Government had not publicly acknowledged a crisis situation. They had taken certain precautions, brought in temporary measures to ease shortages and dealt with new developments on an *ad hoc* basis. Endeavoured to play it cool. Or so it seemed. Now they levelled with us. It was obvious that they must have been planning for months, only awaiting the right psychological moment to take everything over. That moment had clearly come. What we had previously thought of as a free world ended. We could no longer eat, drink, move without permits or coupons. This was full-scale emergency.

Yet nothing proceeds logically. Plans are made only to be

remade to accommodate new and totally unexpected developments. The heat, unpatterned as disseminated sclerosis, attacks
first here, then there. Areas of high temperature suddenly and
inexplicably cool off – or vice versa. Agronomists are doing
everything possible to keep crops coming – taking advantage of
hot-house conditions to force two crops where one had grown
before – frantically playing a kind of agricultural roulette,
gambling on the length of time a specific region might continue
to grow temperate-zone produce.

Mails have long since stopped. And newspapers. And telephones. As a member of a new privileged class, I have been
equipped with a two-way radio and a permit to drive on Government business. Schools have of course closed. An attempt
was made for a time to provide lessons over TV. Thankfully the
looting and rioting seem over. Those desperate gangs of angry
citizens who for some time made life additionally difficult, have
now disappeared. We seem at last to understand that we are all
in this together.

Life is very simple without electricity. I get up with the light
and go to bed as darkness falls. My food supply is still substan-
tial and because of the soybean crop I am all right for water.
Dexter has adapted well to his new life. He is outdoors less than
he used to be and has switched to a mainly vegetable diet without too much difficulty.

Evening. This morning a new order over the radio. All of us
with special driving privileges were asked to report to our zone
garage to have our tires treated with heat-resistant plastic.

I had not been into town for months. I felt rather as one does
on returning home from hospital – that the world is unexpectedly large, with voluminous airy spaces. This was exaggerated
perhaps by the fact that our whole zone had been given over to
soybeans. Everywhere the same rows of green plants – small
pods already formed – march across gardens and boulevards. I

174

was glad to see the climate prove so favourable. But there was little else to make me rejoice as I drove through ominously deserted streets, paint blistering and peeling on fences and houses, while overhead a haze of dust, now always with us, created a green sun.

The prolonged heat has made bleak the little park opposite the garage. A rocky little park, once all mosses and rhododendrons, it is bare now, and brown. I was seeing the day as everyone saw it. Untransmuted.

As I stepped out of my car to speak to the attendant I cursed that I had not brought my insulators. The burning tarmac made me shift rapidly from foot to foot. Anyone from another planet would have wondered at this extraordinary quirk of earthlings. But my feet were forgotten as my eyes alighted a second time on the park across the way. I had never before seen so dazzling and variegated a display of colours. How could there be such prismed brilliance in the range of greys and browns? It was as if the perceiving organ – wherever it is – sensitized by earlier experience, was now correctly tuned for this further perception.

The process was as before: the merest shake and the whole park was 'rainbow, rainbow, rainbow'. A further shake brought the park from *there* to *here*. Interior. But this time the interior space had increased. Doubled. By a kind of instant knowledge that rid me of all doubt, I knew that the garage attendant was seeing it too. *We saw the colours.*

Then, with that slight shift of focus, as if a gelatinous film had moved briefly across my sight, everything slipped back.

I really looked at the attendant for the first time. He was a skinny young man standing up naked inside a pair of loose striped overalls cut off at the knee, *sidney* embroidered in red over his left breast pocket. He was blond, small-boned, with nothing about him to stick in the memory except his clear eyes which at that moment bore an expression of total comprehension.

'You ...' we began together and laughed.

'Have you seen them before?' I asked. But it was rather as one would say 'how do you do' – not so much a question as a salutation.

We looked at each other for a long time, as if committing each other to memory.

'Do you know anyone else?' I said.

'One or two. Three, actually. Do you?'

I shook my head. 'You are the first. Is it ... is it ... always like that?'

'You mean ...?' he gestured towards his heart.

I nodded.

'Yes,' he said. 'Yes, it is.'

There didn't seem anything more to talk about. Your right hand hasn't much to say to your left, or one eye to the other. There was comfort in the experience, if comfort is the word, which it isn't. More as if an old faculty had been extended. Or a new one activated.

Sidney put my car on the hoist and sprayed its tires.

Some time later. I have not seen Sidney again. Two weeks ago when I went back he was not there and as of yesterday, cars have become obsolete. Not that we will use that word publicly. The official word is *suspended.*

Strange to be idle after months of hard labour. A lull only before the boys from the Department of Agriculture come back to prepare the land again. I am pleased that the soybeans are harvested, that I was able to nurse then along to maturity despite the scorching sun, the intermittent plagues and the problems with water. Often the pressure was too low to turn the sprinklers and I would stand, hour after hour, hose in hand, trying to get the most use from the tiny trickle spilling from the nozzle.

Sometimes my heart turns over as I look through the kitchen window and see the plants shrivelled and grotesque, the baked earth scored by a web of fine cracks like the glaze on a plate subjected to too high an oven. Then it comes to me in a flash that of course, the beans are gone, the harvest is over.

The world is uncannily quiet. I don't think anyone had any idea of how much noise even distant traffic made until we were without it. It is rare indeed for vehicles other than Government mini-cars to be seen on the streets. And there are fewer and fewer pedestrians. Those who do venture out move on their thick insulators with the slow gait of rocking-horses. Surreal and alien, they heighten rather than lessen one's sense of isolation. For one *is* isolated. We have grown used to the sight of helicopters like large dragon-flies hovering overhead – addressing us through their P.A. systems, dropping supplies – welcome but impersonal.

Dexter is my only physical contact. He is delighted to have me inside again. The heat is too great for him in the garden and as, officially, he no longer exists, we only go out under cover of dark.

The order to destroy pets, when it came, indicated more clearly than anything that had gone before, that the Government had abandoned hope. In an animal-loving culture, only direct necessity could validate such an order. It fell upon us like a heavy pall.

When the Government truck stopped by for Dexter, I reported him dead. Now that the welfare of so many depends upon our cooperation with authority, law-breaking is a serious offence. But I am not uneasy about breaking this law. As long as he remains healthy and happy, Dexter and I will share our dwindling provisions.

No need to be an ecologist or dependent on non-existent media to know all life is dying and the very atmosphere of our planet is changing radically. Already no birds sing in the hideous hot dawns as the sun, rising through a haze of dust, sheds its curious bronze-green light on a brown world. The trees that once gave us shade stand leafless now in an infernal winter. Yet as if in the masts and riggings of ships, St. Elmo's fire flickers and shines in their high branches, and bioplasmic pyrotechnics light the dying soybeans. I am reminded of how the ghostly form of a limb remains attached to the body from which it has been amputated. And I can't help thinking of all the people who don't see the colours, the practical earth-touchers with only their blunt senses to inform them. I wonder about J. and if, since we last talked, she has perhaps been able to see the colours too. But I think not. After so many years of friendship, surely I would be able to sense her, had she broken through.

Evening...? The heat has increased greatly in the last few weeks – in a quantum leap. This has resulted immediately in two things: a steady rising of the sea level throughout the world – with panic reactions and mild flooding in coastal areas; and, at last, a noticeably higher air temperature. It is causing great physical discomfort.

It was against this probability that the authorities provided us with insulator spray. Like giant cans of pressurized shaving cream. I have shut all rooms but the kitchen and by concentrating my insulating zeal on this one small area, we have managed to keep fairly cool. The word is relative, of course. The radio has stopped giving temperature readings and I have no thermometer. I have filled all cracks and crannies with the foaming plastic, even applied a layer to the exterior wall. There are no baths, of course, and no cold drinks. On the other hand I've abandoned clothes and given Dexter a shave and a haircut. Myself as well. We are a fine pair. Hairless and naked.

When the world state of emergency was declared we didn't need to be told that science had given up. The official line had been that the process would reverse itself as inexplicably as it had begun. The official policy – to hold out as long as possible. With this in mind, task forces worked day and night on survival strategy. On the municipal level, which is all I really knew about, everything that could be centralized was. Telephone exchanges, hydro plants, radio stations became centres around which vital activities took place. Research teams investigated the effects of heat on water mains, sewer pipes, electrical wiring; work crews were employed to prevent, protect or even destroy incipient causes of fire, flood and asphyxiation.

For some time now the city has been zoned. In each zone a large building has been selected, stocked with food, medical supplies and insulating materials. We have been provided with zone maps and an instruction sheet telling us to stay where we are until ordered to move to what is euphemistically called our 'home'. When ordered, we are to load our cars with whatever we still have of provisions and medicines and drive off *at once*. Helicopters have already dropped kits with enough gasoline for the trip and a small packet, somewhat surprisingly labelled 'emergency rations' which contains one cyanide capsule – grim reminder that all may not go as the planners plan. We have been asked to mark our maps, in advance, with the shortest route from our house to our 'home', so that in a crisis we will know what we are doing. These instructions are repeated *ad nauseam* over the radio, along with hearty assurances that everything is under control and that there is no cause for alarm. The Government station is now all that remains of our multimedia. When it is not broadcasting instructions, its mainly pre-recorded tapes sound inanely complacent and repetitive. Evacuation Day, as we have been told again and again, will be announced by whistle blast. Anyone who runs out of food before that or who is in need of medical aid is to use the special gas ration and go 'home' at once.

As a long-time preserver of fruits and vegetables, I hope to hold out until E. Day. When that time comes it will be a sign that broadcasts are no longer possible, that contact can no longer be maintained between the various areas of the community, that the process will not reverse itself in time and that, in fact, our world is well on the way to becoming – oh, wonder of the modern kitchen – a self-cleaning oven.

Spring, Summer, Winter, Fall. What season is it after all? I sense the hours by some inner clock. I have applied so many layers of insulating spray that almost no heat comes through from outside. But we have to have air and the small window I have left exposed acts like a furnace. Yet through it I see the dazzling colours; sense my fellow-men.

Noon. The sun is hidden directly overhead. The world is topaz. I see it through the minute eye of my window. I, the perceiving organ that peers through the house's only aperture. We are one, the house and I – parts of some vibrating sensitive organism in which Dexter plays his differentiated but integral role. The light enters us, dissolves us. We are the golden motes in the jewel.

Midnight. The sun is directly below. Beneath the burning soles of my arching feet it shines, a globe on fire. Its rays penetrate the earth. Upward beaming, they support and sustain us. We are held aloft, a perfectly balanced ball in the jet of a golden fountain. Light, dancing, infinitely upheld.

Who knows how much later. I have just 'buried' Dexter.

This morning I realized this hot little cell was no longer a possible place for a dog.

I had saved one can of dog food against this day. As I opened it Dexter's eyes swivelled in the direction of so unexpected and delicious a smell. He struggled to his feet, joyous, animated.

The old Dexter. I was almost persuaded to delay, to wait and see if the heat subsided. What if tomorrow we awakened to rain? But something in me, stronger than this wavering self, carried on with its purpose.

He sat up, begging, expectant.

I slipped the meat out of the can.

'You're going to have a really good dinner,' I said, but as my voice was unsteady, I stopped.

I scooped a generous portion of the meat into his dish and placed it on the floor. He was excited, and as always when excited about food, he was curiously ceremonial, unhurried – approaching his dish and backing away from it, only to approach it again at a slightly different angle. As if the exact position was of the greatest importance. It was one of his most amusing and endearing characteristics. I let him eat his meal in his own leisurely and appreciative manner and then, as I have done so many times before, I fed him his final *bonne bouche* by hand. The cyanide pill, provided by a beneficent Government for me, went down in a gulp.

I hadn't expected it to be so sudden. Life and death so close. His small frame convulsed violently, then collapsed. Simultaneously, as if synchronized, the familiar 'shake' occurred in my vision. Dexter glowed brightly, whitely, like phosphorus. In that dazzling, light-filled moment he was no longer a small dead dog lying there. I could have thought him a lion, my sense of scale had so altered. His beautiful body blinded me with its fires.

With the second 'shake' his consciousness must have entered mine for I felt a surge in my heart as if his loyalty and love had flooded it. And like a kind of ground bass, I was aware of scents and sounds I had not known before. Then a great peace filled me – an immense space, light and sweet – and I realized that this was death. Dexter's death.

But how describe what is beyond description?

As the fires emanating from his slight frame died down, glowed weakly, residually, I put on my insulators and carried his body into the now fever-hot garden. I laid him on what had been at one time an azalea bed. I was unable to dig a grave in the baked earth or to cover him with leaves. But there are no predators now to pick the flesh from his bones. Only the heat which will, in time, desiccate it.

I returned to the house, opening the door as little as possible to prevent the barbs and briars of burning air from entering with me. I sealed the door from inside with foam sealer.

The smell of the canned dog food permeated the kitchen. It rang in my nostrils. Olfactory chimes, lingering, delicious. I was intensely aware of Dexter. Dexter immanent. I contained him as simply as a dish contains water. But the simile is not exact. For I missed his physical presence. One relies on the physical more than I had known. My hands sought palpable contact. The flesh forgets slowly.

Idly, abstractedly, I turned on the radio. I seldom do now as the batteries are low and they are my last. Also, there is little incentive. Broadcasts are intermittent and I've heard the old tapes over and over.

But the Government station was on the air. I tuned with extreme care and placed my ear close to the speaker. A voice, faint, broken by static, sounded like that of the Prime Minister.

'... all human beings can do, your Government has done for you.' (Surely not a political speech *now?*) 'But we have failed. Failed to hold back the heat. Failed to protect ourselves against it; to protect you against it. It is with profound grief that I send this farewell message to you all.' I realized that this, too, had been pre-recorded, reserved for the final broadcast. 'Even now, let us not give up hope ...'

And then, blasting through the speech, monstrously loud in the stone-silent world, the screech of the whistle summoning us 'home'. I could no longer hear the P.M.'s words.

I began automatically, obediently, to collect my few remaining foodstuffs, reaching for a can of raspberries, the last of the crop to have grown in my garden when dawns were dewy and cool and noon sun fell upon us like golden pollen. My hand stopped in mid-air.

I would not go 'home'.

The whistle shrilled for a very long time. A curious great steam-driven cry – man's last. Weird that our final utterance should be this anguished inhuman wail.

The end. Now that it is virtually too late, I regret not having kept a daily record. Now that the part of me that writes has become nearly absorbed, I feel obliged to do the best I can.

I am down to the last of my food and water. Have lived on little for some days – weeks, perhaps. How can one measure passing time? Eternal time grows like a tree, its roots in my heart. If I lie on my back I see winds moving in its high branches and a chorus of birds is singing in its leaves. The song is sweeter than any music I have ever heard.

My kitchen is as strange as I am myself. Its walls bulge with many layers of spray. It is without geometry. Like the inside of an eccentric Styrofoam coconut. Yet, with some inner eye, I see its intricate mathematical structure. It is as ordered and no more random than an atom.

My face is unrecognizable in the mirror. Wisps of short damp hair. Enormous eyes. I swim in their irises. Could I drown in the pits of their pupils?

Through my tiny window when I raise the blind, a dead world shines. Sometimes dust storms fill the air with myriad particles burning bright and white as the lion body of Dexter. Sometimes great clouds swirl, like those from which saints receive revelations.

The colours are almost constant now. There are times when, light-headed, I dance a dizzying dance, feel part of that whirling incandescent matter – what I might once have called inorganic matter!

On still days the blameless air, bright as a glistening wing, hangs over us, hangs its extraordinary beneficence over us.

We are together now, united, indissoluble. Bonded.

Because there is no expectation, there is no frustration.

Because there is nothing we can have, there is nothing we can want.

We are hungry of course. Have cramps and weakness. But they are as if in *another body*. Our body is inviolate. Inviolable.

We share one heart.

We are one with the starry heavens and our bodies are stars.

Inner and outer are the same. A continuum. The water in the locks is level. We move to a higher water. A high sea.

A ship could pass through.

(1979)

Acknowledgements

Many of these stories have appeared in previous publications:

'The Neighbour', *Preview*, 1942
'The Green Bird', *Preview*, 1942
'The Lord's Plan', *Preview*, 1942
'Miracles', *Preview*, 1944
'George', *Reading*, 1946
'The Woman', *Here and Now*, 1947; *In the Hills*, 2001
'As One Remembers a Dream'. First publication, *The Sun and the Moon and Other Fictions*, Anansi, 1973
'The Glass Box'. First publication, *The Sun and the Moon and Other Fictions*', Anansi, 1973
'Victoria', *Tamarack Review*, 1976
'Unless the Eye Catch Fire', *Malahat Review*, 1979
'Birthday', *Malahat Review*, 1985
'Mme Bourgé Dreams of *Brésil*', *Cross-Country Writers*, 1987
'Nãrada's Lesson' (a short story based on a Hindu tale), *The Monkey King*, edited by Griffin Ondaatje, 1995
'The Sky Tree', *Malahat Review*, 1996
'Fever', *Exile*, 1999
'Even the Sun ...', *Malahat Review*, 1999
'A Kind of Fiction', *Descant*, 2000
'The Blind Men and the Elephant' (a short play based on a fable by the Persian poet, Jalaludin Rumi), *The Ottawa Citizen*, 2001

BARBARA PEDRICK

P.K. Page has written some of the best poems published in Canada for over five decades. In addition to winning the Governor General's award for poetry in 1957, she was appointed a Companion of the Order of Canada in 1999. She is the author of more than a dozen books, which include ten volumes of poetry, a novel, selected short stories, three books for children, and a memoir entitled *Brazilian Journal* based on her extended stay in Brazil with her late husband Arthur Irwin who served as the Canadian Ambassador to Brazil from 1957 to 1959. A two-volume edition of her collected poems, *The Hidden Room* (PQL), was published in 1997.

She also paints under the name P.K. Irwin. She has mounted one-woman shows in Mexico and Canada, and has been exhibited in various group shows. Her work is represented in the permanent collections of the National Gallery of Canada, the Art Gallery of Ontario and the Victoria Art Gallery, among others.

P.K. Page was born in England and brought up on the Canadian prairies. She has lived in the Maritimes and Montreal. After years abroad in Australia, Brazil and Mexico, she now makes her permanent home in Victoria, British Columbia.